Tess laughed, shaking

She leaned back in her chair and gave him the once-over. "I know you know me better than that. You don't really think that I'd allow anyone to 'order' me to do anything." She flashed him a grin and a raised eyebrow that said she had his number. "Even though I hear that you're really good at it."

"Well, I am really good at it." Adam kept his eyes locked on hers as he rounded her desk, stopping just close enough to feel the heat generated by their proximity and chemistry. Pure chemical reaction. Spontaneous combustion.

"I'm a decisive man, Tess."

"Yes. I am aware." With her heels on, they were almost eye-to-eye, mouth-to-mouth, chest-to-breast. "You are also private, loyal, harsh, fair and intense." Her voice lowered and he leaned in closer to catch every word.

"And you're very sexy...".

* * *

Taking on the Billionaire by Robin Covington
is part of the Redhawk Reunion series.

Dear Reader,

Family is messy and complicated and even more so when you are separated for fifteen years. Adam Redhawk has been there, done that and has all the T-shirts!

In *Taking on the Billionaire*, Adam is trying to do it all: launch the biggest app for his tech company and reconnect with the brother and sister he finally found after their family was ripped apart. And the person who is there to help him with all of this is Tess Lynch, the woman he should not want and the woman with the agenda that might just cost him everything.

I cannot tell you how much fun I had writing the sexy, emotional roller-coaster ride that Adam and Tess take on their journey. I can honestly say that I have the best job in the world.

And the story of a Native American family reunited after being torn apart is a dream come true for me. When you grow up separated from your roots, the reconnection with the history that runs through your veins is a painful and glorious gift. The Redhawk Reunion series—the stories of Adam, Sarina and Roan—is my love letter to my ancestors.

Thank you for reading Adam and Tess's story... The rest of the Redhawk saga is coming your way.

Xoxo,

Robin

ROBIN COVINGTON

———

TAKING ON THE BILLIONAIRE

ISBN-13: 978-1-335-20954-2

Taking on the Billionaire

Recycling programs
for this product may
not exist in your area.

This edition published by arrangement with Harlequin Books S.A.

For questions and comments about the quality of this book, please contact us at CustomerService@Harlequin.com.

Harlequin Enterprises ULC
22 Adelaide St. West, 40th Floor
Toronto, Ontario M5H 4E3, Canada
www.Harlequin.com

Printed in U.S.A.

A *USA TODAY* bestselling author, **Robin Covington** loves to explore the theme of fooling around and falling in love in her books. When she's not writing, she's collecting tasty man candy, indulging in a little comic book geek love, hoarding red nail polish and stalking Chris Evans.

Robin is a 2016 RITA® Award nominee, and her books have won the National Readers' Choice and Golden Leaf Awards and finaled for the RT Reviewers' Choice Award, the Booksellers' Best Award and the Award of Excellence.

She lives in Maryland with her hilarious husband, her two brilliant children (they get it from her, of course!), and her beloved fur babies, Dutch and Dixie Joan Wilder. Drop her a line at robin@robincovington romance.com—she always writes back.

Visit her Author Profile page at Harlequin.com for more titles.

You can also find Robin Covington on Facebook, along with other Harlequin Desire authors, at Facebook.com/harlequindesireauthors!

To my editor, Charles Griemsman, and my agent, Nalini Akolekar: thank you for making my dreams of becoming a Harlequin author a reality.

Patrick, Rory and Fiona—the best family in the world. I'm so lucky that you're mine.

One

Tess Lynch was a distraction.

A sexy, smart, competent, mouth-wateringly tempting distraction.

For the millionth time since he'd first met her, Adam Redhawk regretted his decision to take the office that was glass on three sides. Everyone had told him that this office, with its commanding prize of place in the corporate headquarters of Redhawk/ Ling, was the best way to announce to the world that he was the CEO of a billion-dollar tech company.

Now he'd give at least a million to get one damn solid wall.

His luxury corporate fishbowl gave him zero opportunity to get his act together before his favorite redheaded private investigator sauntered into his space and plopped a thick file on the center of his desk. And God knew that Adam needed every second to get his act together when it came to Tess Lynch. He spared a glance at the pile of papers she'd tossed down, the sprawl of folders out of place on the immaculate desktop, but he couldn't resist the compulsion to return his gaze back to her face and the sparkling flash of her golden-jade eyes.

She was laughing at him, dammit.

Of course she was.

"Good afternoon, Ms. Lynch." He glanced at his watch, knowing full well what time it was but taking the extra few seconds to school his expression before looking at her again. Her auburn curls were loose today and she wore a body-skimming dark pink dress that ended just above the knee. The entire outfit looked like it was specifically made to showcase her full, voluptuous figure. Tess reminded him of the classic film star Rita Hayworth, a favorite of his adoptive mother. Bold and self-assured, Tess was… breathtaking. "You're late."

She laughed, tossing off her jacket and his censure at the same time. "Only fifteen minutes."

"That is *still* late."

He wanted to keep the steel in his voice, wanted to keep the necessary distance between them, *needed* to keep believing that he didn't want her. But it was impossible when she slinked around the edge of his desk until there was barely an arm's length between them. This close he could see the splash of freckles across her nose and smell the scent of her, soft and citrus sharp. Everything in his body went on high alert and he marveled that she didn't feel the heat wafting off him in pulse-pounding waves.

Temptation. If he looked the word up in the dictionary, she'd be there, complete with red-gold hair, freckles and a sly, kissable grin.

"You're right," she agreed, surprising him with her quick acquiescence. Usually they sparred a bit longer before one of them begrudgingly conceded temporary defeat and they proceeded to take care of business. "But I knew you had a meeting with Justin right before this and he *always* starts fifteen minutes late and goes over by the same amount." Tess leaned against his desk, her body language communicating just how much she didn't care if he was irritated with her being late to the meeting. He watched as she picked up the pair of drumsticks on his desk and lazily twirled them between her slim fingers, the look in her eyes daring him to stop her. "So, Mr. Redhawk, I'm not late. I'm right on time."

Adam couldn't argue with her. Her position was logical and fact based, two things that always made sense to him. And her lips twisting in a sexy "you know I'm right" smile crumbled any argument he was going to make.

He grinned and nodded in concession while he reached out and took his sticks out of her hands and placed them back on the desk. "One day I'm going to take Justin's watch and reset it so that he'll be on time for once."

"That won't work. You'd have better luck trying to change the tide."

That was true. His best friend and business partner marched to his own internal clock. He was never going to change.

"How did the two of you ever become friends?" Tess asked, shifting over toward the grouping of personal photos on the low table behind his desk. She leaned over, focusing on one of Justin and him at Stanford. Two smiling idiots, stupid enough to think they could quit academia and make their dream come true.

The idiots had done all right.

"It was in the campus security lockup. Justin talked them into letting us go with just a warning." Adam shook his head at the memory. What a pair of dumbass, know-it-all jerks they'd been back then.

"I bet he did." Tess laughed, shifting to peek up at him between glossy auburn curls. "What did you guys do to get busted by the cops?"

"I'll never tell."

"I can find out, you know." She murmured, "It *is* my job."

Tess touched the photo and Adam watched her.

The way she moved so confidently in his space was mesmerizing. Tess was gorgeous, her body curvy and sexy, but it was the way she owned her place in the world that kept him awake at night. It was her take-no-prisoners bravado that kept him hard and wanting anytime she was near. When she straightened and looked at him over his shoulder, he almost forgot that they were in an office exposed to all of his employees. The office where he was supposed to be running his billion-dollar company and not yearning to kiss this woman, to taste this woman, to possess this woman.

What was this thing between them? Tess Lynch was not the kind of woman who usually caught his eye. She was secretive and elusive, mouthy and brash, and owned her blatant brand of sexuality. She was also decisively stubborn but also changed her moods and mind as quickly as a hummingbird flew. Tess Lynch was a walking danger sign that he should heed but spent way too much time figuring out ways to ignore. She did not fit in the way he wanted his world to function, but he found himself caring less and less.

A few months ago he'd taken the referral from a friend of his and hired Tess to find his younger brother and sister. They'd all been taken from their parents and separated in an illegal adoption twenty-four years ago, and now he'd finally made good on the promise that six-year-old Adam had made to himself and his ancestors. Tess had been successful and located both Sarina and Roan and now she was here to deliver the final report.

But while the job he initially hired her to do was over, he was glad to have another reason to keep her around a little while longer. Which was insane because if he was right, the problem he needed her to help solve could take down his company and everything he'd fought to achieve.

Adam needed to focus. He'd asked for this meeting because he needed to take quick action if he was going to save the company he created. Adam turned away from her, needing to break the connection and regroup.

He spied the folders on the desk and tapped a finger on the papers. "What's this?"

"The final report…" she paused, tilting her head to the side, watching him closely "…and copies of everything I found while I was searching for your family. Court records. Newspaper clippings. Educational, job and criminal records. The last twenty years condensed on paper and a USB drive." He raised an eyebrow in question and Tess shrugged. "I know you didn't ask for all of that extra stuff but I thought you might like to have it. It might connect some dots."

Damn. Well, he'd asked. And wasn't this just like jumping from the corporate frying pan into the fire of messy family relations?

His hand hovered over the top folder while he

played chicken with his past. He'd spent a ton of money and a lot of time to find his lost brother and sister and the answers to all of the questions that had tormented him for the last twenty-four years were sitting on his desk reduced to words and pixels.

Finally forcing himself to open it, he was greeted by his own face looking back at him in two pictures. The first was his current headshot and the other was when he was six years old, the photo his adoptive parents had first seen when they were picking out a kid to give a better life to. Hardened brown eyes that knew way too much about the shit life could throw at you stared back at him from the page. Adam shut the folder. He knew the rest of his story.

The other two packets contained similar but completely different histories. His brother and sister, Sarina and Roan, flashed across his line of vision in a stream of photos and facts and data about what had happened to them after they'd been separated and sent to different families. Different states. Different lives. Different trauma but the same hard expression stared back at him in the photographs. He was anxious to read every word and sickened by the sensation that he was prying into things he had no business knowing.

Things he had paid Tess to find out when he'd hired her to find them.

Things he'd know firsthand if their lives had turned out differently.

Adam slammed the folder shut and tossed it with more force than he intended, causing a couple of pens to shoot off the other side of the desk onto the hardwood floor. He cursed under his breath and took a step to pick them up but the firm press of Tess's hand on his arm stopped him cold. He glanced down at where she touched him, her warmth raising goose bumps on his own skin, and then lifted his eyes to meet her gaze. He'd expected pity so the open, clear expression of understanding on her face surprised him.

"Adam, I gave them both the same information. You're all starting at the same place, with the same facts about each other."

He shifted his arm and Tess's grip slid until their hands fit together. The touch of their palms was electric, sharp but totally right. They stared at each other, his eyes drifting down to her lips as they parted on a stutter as she temporarily lost her train of thought.

"Family is hard," she whispered, voice catching on the last part with whatever baggage she brought along with her.

Oh hell. Adam squeezed his eyes shut to the gut punch her words delivered. He'd never been good with the family who'd raised him and now he had a long-lost sister and brother to make some kind of future with. What the hell had he been thinking?

"If it helps, the three of you are more alike than you'd think," she continued, her voice stronger, soothing and laced with humor. "You all ride motorcycles. Fast ones. Loud ones. And no European crotch rockets, either. You people are a Harley family. It's like it's imprinted on your DNA or something."

This surprised a laugh out of him and something tight in his throat broke loose. Tess's eyes widened as she tilted her head to the side with the unspoken question.

"Our dad had a crappy Harley. I remember riding around with him on the Qualla Boundary." The memory was one of the few he still had that felt real. Most of that time felt like he made it up or that it had happened to someone else. Twenty-four years was a long time. "I guess it is in our DNA."

Adam released her hand, breaking their connection, and walked over to the windows looking out over the wooded tech campus. This part of California was beautiful, nothing like what he could remember of the lush, blue-tinged mystery of the mountains of his boyhood home. But it was gorgeous in its own way. He'd built something here with Justin, a company that employed a lot of people and had the potential to help many, many more.

He'd created a really good life for himself. It would only be better with his brother and sister in it.

But while he wanted to sit down and devour every bit of the information about his family, now was not the time. The future of his company was on the line and he needed Tess and her skills to save it.

Redhawk/Ling had a launch in eight weeks, the app that would make or break this company, and they had a problem. A very big problem and he needed her help.

He turned to Tess and finally got to the main reason he'd asked her to meet him today.

"Tess, I didn't ask you here just to get the final report. I need to hire you for another job. Somebody from inside Redhawk/Ling is trying to take us down and I want to hire you to find out who it is."

Two

It was as if the universe was finally on her side.

Tess tried not to do a happy dance at the revelation that Adam Redhawk was keeping her on for another job. Just when she was wondering what excuse she was going to use to continue their contact, he invited her right in.

And ensured that she would get her revenge.

She couldn't afford to give anything away; this development was too crucial. So, Tess got her excitement under control and focused on the business at hand.

"I'm flattered that you think I can do the job but I don't know much about corporate espionage."

She let the silence spread out between them. Adam was a thoughtful man and he wasn't going to speak in haste. It had served him well throughout his life, keeping him insulated and beyond the hurt and pain life wanted to inflict. Tess had admired it from the first moment she'd met him although it had made him a very difficult mark.

It also made him intriguing, mesmerizing, completely intoxicating. Adam Redhawk was a constant temptation to her. He made her want things, made her want him. In her bed, inside her body but also in her life. He was sexy, whip-smart, strong and honorable. He was the kind of man every woman hoped they would find but he was also the one that none of them could capture.

Adam never had a lack of women in his bed. Not that he bragged about it; she'd had to do her own digging on that point. And by all accounts from those who knew, his still waters ran deep and dirty in the bedroom. A staple on the "top ten sexiest bachelors" lists, Mr. Redhawk was a definite catch, but he refused to take the bait. Nobody stayed over. Nobody lingered in his life for long.

He was a challenge and Tess thrived on a challenge. She knew how to use her looks, her body and sexuality to get what she wanted. But she'd not pursued him, not taken that tack in her plan to get closer to him. He wanted her; she knew it. She wanted him; they both knew it. But she *liked* him and that feeling would not help her do what she needed to do. Those feelings would only lead to complications that she didn't want or need.

So, the fantasy of Adam taking her, rough and tumble on his immaculate desk, had never become a reality.

A regret that had kept her up more than one night.

Adam continued his pitch, oblivious to where her mind had wandered. "You can find people. You blew apart the maze of bureaucratic bullshit and found my sister and brother so I think you can find out who is trying to ruin this company."

Tess nodded toward the long leather sofa in his office. "This feels like a long story. Mind if I sit?"

"Of course."

Tess took a seat, watching Adam prowl the perimeter of his office, pacing back and forth in front of the window as if he was imprisoned here in his high-end Silicon Valley prison. Maybe he was. Adam Redhawk had grown up with high expectations imposed on him and now he'd shouldered ones of his own making. When he spoke, it was controlled and even but she could hear the undercurrent of fury.

"In eight weeks we are launching an app that will revolutionize the world." Adam glanced at her, his eyebrows raised in question. "All of this is confidential in accordance with your previously signed agreement. You understand?"

"Of course. You can count on my discretion," she

answered, not taking any offense at his question. Redhawk/Ling was a company that made dreams an actual reality and it was only natural that they would protect them like children.

"This app will make it possible for any device to communicate and work together with any other device. You can interchange apps, programs, music, documents…the operating system will no longer matter."

Tess sat up a little straighter, her brain trying to wrap around this information. "This is going to make you rich." She shook her head, laughing at the stupidity of her statement. "It is going to make you richer. Ridiculously rich."

"Justin says that that there is 'fuck you money' and that this will be 'I can pay someone to fuck you money.'"

"Justin would say that." Tess chuckled, her mind turning the situation over in her mind. "So, someone is trying to steal information about the app?"

Adam nodded, coming over to sit next to her on the couch. He had his sleeves rolled up and when he leaned on his knees, his forearms flexed in that sexy way that got her attention every time. He was in great shape. His muscles shifting underneath his impeccably tailored suits made her mind wander to speculation about what he looked like under all that fabric.

Not that she had to leave it all up to her imagination. He'd been photographed when he'd raced in a triathlon last year. Miles and miles of taut, bronzed skin over muscles formed through years of running and hiking and competition. Her heart rate sped up and her palms itched to reach out and touch him again like she had just a few moments ago. That had been unexpected since she made it a point to avoid physical contact with Adam. But he'd looked so vulnerable, so lost that all the rules flew out the big floor-to-ceiling windows.

Adam answered her question. "Someone is trying to ruin the launch. Not sure if they want to try and reverse engineer it or just steal our thunder. Either way, we cannot afford for that to happen. Justin and I have reinvested a significant portion of the company's money into this app, so it has to work."

"Or you lose everything?"

"Everything that counts. Besides our investment, we'd have to lay off people. These folks stood by us when we were just two crazy college dropouts working out of the back of a warehouse. I don't want to let people down." Adam shifted next to her, their knees brushing as he faced her head-on. His eyes were dark with the intensity of his emotions and he leaned in close enough for her to smell the exotic woodsy scent of his aftershave. "I need someone on this that I can trust, Tess. You're smart and I know you can do this."

Tess tried not to cringe every time he mentioned the word *trust*. He really shouldn't. He had no idea how much he shouldn't. "I'm just a P.I. I'm a great P.I. but I don't know anything about corporate espionage."

"I'm not worried about it. You're a quick study and I don't need you to know my business. You know people and what would make someone steal from me. That's what I need." Adam paused, before adding with a wink, "Besides, I know you, which means I don't have to get to know anyone else."

"I forgot—you don't like people."

"Not as a rule, no." Adam shrugged, pulled a piece of paper out of his shirt pocket and held it out to her. "Justin and I wrote down a list of people who we think are worth looking into. It should get you started."

Tess ignored the way he assumed she would be taking the case and took the paper, opening it to read the names written down. Her heart kicked up a beat when she read the first one, convinced that the universe was sending her a signal.

"Franklin Thornton? He's at the top of your list?"

Adam nodded, his eyes narrowed in suspicion and anger. It was no secret that there was no love lost between Adam and his adoptive father.

"Franklin would love to see Redhawk/Ling crash like the Hindenburg. He also has the juice to make it worth someone's time to sell our asses out." Adam reached out and grabbed a cup of coffee, took a sip and grimaced before putting down the mug. "Franklin is always at the top of the list. That's not paranoia. It's just business to him and it is what he does. Putting me in my place is the cherry on top of the goddamn sundae."

Tess was very much aware of how Franklin Thornton ate people up and spit them out. She knew the way that he trashed people's dreams, destroyed their hope and betrayed their trust. She knew what happened to people who ended up on the shit end of Franklin Thornton; they ended up broken, insane with grief and oblivious to the two daughters that needed them to be their dad.

Franklin Thornton ruined people but he also created enemies.

He'd created Tess Lynch and she'd spent the last ten years looking for the perfect chance to get close to him and bring him down. And it didn't matter if she had to go through the man sitting next to her to get to him; she was going to get him.

There was only one answer to Adam's question.

"I'll need an office here, access to security files and IT support."

Three

The files were everywhere.

Adam tried not to twitch at the absolute shitshow his office had become. Stacks of folders were scattered across the table, three laptops were open with spreadsheets covering all of the screens. And coffee cups and empty food containers littered the coffee table and piled up in the trashcan.

Adam didn't want to be the guy who was bothered by the disorder and chaos but he was one hundred percent *that* guy.

Justin was not.

"How did we end up with so many weirdos working here?" Justin asked, lounging back with his size twelve Converse Chucks kicked up on the coffee table. He held a folder in his hands, reading over the reports Tess had compiled on the most likely employees of Redhawk/Ling. "What the hell is LARP-ing? Is that the costume thing? The Comic-Con stuff?"

"It's live-action-role-playing." Tess strolled by him and nudged his feet to the floor, shooting Adam a secret smile. "It's what you would have been doing if you'd actually had the guts to get out from behind the computer screen in your parents' basement and go out and meet real girls."

Justin sat up straight and looked absolutely offended. "I was not in my parents' basement. I had a computer in my room." He motioned to Adam. "Do I have to put up with this?"

Tess scoffed. "If you yuck on somebody else's yum, you get what you get."

Adam snorted and grabbed the file from Justin. "Yeah, Justin, stop yucking on—" he read the name off the folder "—Bryan Lane's yum."

"He's not our guy anyway," Tess interjected, plucking the file from Adam's hand.

Their fingers brushed; their eyes locked on each other and everything else in the room disappeared. He stared at her, zeroing in on the way her body swayed into his. He knew how it was; gravity had nothing on the pull of Tess Lynch.

"How do you know?" Justin inquired, sifting through the stack of files and trying to pretend like he wasn't staring at the two of them. "What are you looking for? What does a traitor look like?"

Tess's gaze lingered on his for a moment longer and then she transferred all her attention to Justin. Adam felt the loss as a physical pang, deep in his gut. And if he zoomed in closely on his emotions, he'd acknowledge that jealousy was in the mix too. But he wasn't zooming in on anything except the task at hand, right now.

"They look like you and me and Estelle," she said, mentioning Adam's long-time and highly beloved personal assistant. "Or that beautiful boy at the corner coffee shop with all of the tattoos."

"Felix. His name is Felix." Adam spoke without thinking, waving off the extended, curious looks from Tess and Justin. "He takes the time to remember my name and my order. I remember his."

"Okay, yes, Felix," Tess agreed. "It would be great if they walked around with a big *T* on their chest or a mustache to twirl like a villain. But, they don't. So, you have to look for an area of exploitation, usually debt, sex or family. It will be a miracle if the IT guys found evidence on the company computers. I'd be shocked if someone was so dumb or brazen. So, I need to look deeper."

"File by file," Adam observed.

"Person by person," Tess answered, pointing to the stacks on the table. "But I'll find them, whoever they are."

Estelle Conway appeared in the doorway, her expression wary. She glanced back over her shoulder, angling her wheelchair across the opening and effectively blocking whoever was behind her. "Mr. Thornton is here to see you, Mr. Redhawk."

Adam went rigid while Justin shot into movement. There was a flurry of arms and legs and thunderous muttering as he rose from the couch in a cascade of paper and folders and advanced toward Estelle.

"What the fuck does he want?" Justin asked, his typically smooth voice ragged with anger.

"I *want* to fucking talk to Adam." Franklin Thornton answered as he pushed past Estelle and barreled through the door, jamming Estelle's chair into the door frame with a metallic thud and bang. His voice was calm and even, in contrast to his physical aggression and demanding movements.

He was a handsome man, his tall frame still broad in the shoulders with a power that hinted at his college football player past. But one look in his eyes told you the truth behind his money and power. It wasn't that he was fouled by hatred or rage. Franklin Thornton was dead inside. He didn't care enough about the people around him to worry about hurting them; you couldn't harm a thing, an object. Adam had learned early that his adoption had had its reasons and none of them involved him or his welfare. He was around because he was useful to Franklin and nothing more. Everything was that complicated and that simple with his adoptive father.

"Mr. Redhawk, I'm sorry," Estelle began to apologize for what she clearly thought was her failure for this man barging his way into the office.

Adam wasn't having it.

He stepped forward and stood in front of Franklin, using his own bulk to block any further progress into the office, any progress toward the work they were doing in here. Adam didn't raise his voice; he'd learned early and often to keep complete control of his reactions, to deny his opponent the opposing show of force they tried to incite.

"Franklin, you need to apologize to Estelle."

He was ignored as he expected, the other man's lips curling into a grin. "Hello, Adam. You've been ignoring my calls."

"If I'd known that answering would have prevented you from showing up here today, I would have…" He considered his options. "I still wouldn't have answered." Adam crossed his arms over his chest and dug in. "Apologize to Estelle. Now. I'm not asking."

Franklin considered him, his gaze never leaving Adam's face. "I apologize."

It was as good as he was going to get. Adam nodded at Estelle, his smile communicating his own apology. He waited until she'd left before he turned back towards Franklin, dropping the smile entirely.

"Whatever you're here for, the answer is 'no,' 'none of your business,' and 'get out.'"

"All of the above," Justin added.

"That too," Adam agreed.

"Cute." Franklin sneered. "I'm here to find out why you have a redhead with big tits asking questions about me."

Franklin's tone was ambivalent but the words hit Adam like a sledgehammer and it took most of his will to not react physically to his words. However, the spark of interest in his adoptive father's eyes told him that he wasn't holding his poker face as well as he usually did. A guttural sound of outrage behind him communicated that Tess wasn't maintaining her cool either. Franklin's eyes slid from Adam's face to look beyond him, to where Tess was standing.

His eyes raked over her before he spoke. "Well, they weren't wrong about the tits."

"Shut your mouth," Adam warned, facing off with Franklin with a shove to his chest before Adam turned and walked toward the fuming Tess.

Now he knew what she looked like when she was pissed and it was so not the right time for him to linger on the fact that she was gorgeous. Anger raised the pink in her cheeks and made her eyes flash a poisonous green.

He never wanted to kiss her more than he did right this instant.

He never wanted to keep Franklin away from someone more than he did in this instant.

"Tess," he murmured as he reached out and grabbed her hand. She tensed, attempting to get him to let her go as she peered over his shoulder, the venom shooting out of her glare like a laser. If it had been leveled at anyone other than Franklin Thornton her opponent would be cowering in a corner, but Adam guessed that Franklin was giving as good as he got. Letting these two at each other would be a very bad idea. He tugged her in closer and leaned down to murmur, his voice pitched low and edged with a warning that he wasn't going to argue about this. "Don't."

At his demand, she stopped resisting him, her eyes snapping to meet his with the sizzling impact of a lightning bolt hitting too close to the mark. Tess wanted to fight. Her reaction was visceral, a tremble of tension that ran up and down her body and hitched her breath with every inhale. Adam slid his hand around her wrist, letting his fingers soothe her with the gentlest touch against her rapidly fluttering pulse point. Franklin got him riled too, pushed buttons he didn't even know he had, but her reaction was strange, more than just anger over his words, and prompted a million questions in his mind. Questions that would wait until later. Right now, he wanted to put as much distance between Franklin and Tess as he could manage.

"Tess, go make sure that Estelle is okay," he asked. She hesitated, her refusal poised on the edge of the tensed hard line of her lips. "Please, baby, just do this."

The unexpected endearment shocked him as it slid past his lips and she was now utterly focused on him. He would have bet money that the world had ground to a damn halt except for the electric current running between the two of them. Tess didn't look angry, didn't look like she objected, her expression was more shocked pleasure and sharp interest than anything else and he wondered what her reaction would be if he tugged her even closer and tasted her mouth. Only the knowledge that Franklin was watching, a viper in his house, kept him from acting on the impulse.

"Please."

His one-word plea broke the spell and spurred her into action. He took in the stiffening of her muscles and the quizzical, lingering glance aimed at him. Then she was gone with a nod and a determined stride past Franklin and out the door. She didn't even spare his adoptive father a glance, but she didn't shrink away, either. Proud and defiant. The Tess he knew and wanted way too much.

"So, who is she, Adam? You're not screwing your help now these days, are you?" Franklin tsked and shook his head. "That doesn't seem like you at all."

Adam took two long strides and then he was toe-to-toe with the man who'd given him a roof and an education but never any affection or acceptance. "Don't ever talk about her like that again."

"So, who is she? What is she doing for you? Why is she asking questions about me?"

"Are you worried about what she'll find out?" Adam replied.

"That's not an answer to my question," Franklin insisted.

"That's all you're going to get so you can leave. I'll have a member of my security staff walk you out," Adam said, nodding toward the burly man in a dark suit now standing in his office doorway.

Franklin followed the path of his attention and glanced over his shoulder, the smirk on his mouth more amused than angry when he turned back.

"No need. I got the answers I wanted anyway." Franklin swept his eyes over the rest of the office, his gaze taking in all of the papers and files. "This office is a mess. No wonder your company is in trouble."

Adam didn't flinch at the icy coldness in Franklin's tone. He was used to him bashing his business, his skill, his ambition, and he was well versed in not giving him the satisfaction of knowing that it pissed him off.

And it infuriated him that the rejection by this man still hurt a little.

Not enough to get him to become the man Franklin wanted him to be but enough to keep him from giving up from his dreams. From giving up and letting down the people who believed in him. He had a lot of people depending on him and he wasn't going to let them down.

Adam waited until Franklin had exited his office and Justin had secured the door behind him before grabbing the nearest object and hurling it across the room. The mug hit the wall, created a significant crater in the dry wall and shattered and scattered across his hardwood floors.

"Man, you just broke the wall," Justin said, walking toward Adam with his hands raised in a placating gesture that made Adam roll his eyes.

"Yeah. Yeah, I'm sorry. I just…"

"You lost your shit." Justin pointed at the mess. "I mean, you're the CEO so you can break the wall if you want to break the wall…"

Adam ground his teeth and searched for words that could shatter the rage haze induced by Franklin.

All he could manage was another lame apology. "I think I threw your mug. I'm sorry."

Justin waved him off, crossing the room while making a show of sidestepping the large shards of ceramic on the floor. "Adam, just shut up already. I'm glad to see you lose your cool for once."

"Losing my cool is unproductive."

"It's also human and a relief to see that you're not actually a robot. I just can't believe that you haven't punched Franklin by now."

Adam knelt down, casting a glance up at his best friend as he picked up the larger pieces of ceramic. They'd known each for a long time and Justin was one of the few people who knew everything that Adam could remember about his life before coming to California and what he couldn't forget about what had happened once he'd arrived.

"It's not like I haven't thought about it," Adam admitted, rising up to toss the pieces into the trash. "Helene would lose her mind if we ended up in the ER and on the front page of the papers."

"Or she could have told her husband not to be a dick," Justin said, shrugging in an apology that didn't look like he meant it at all. His best friend wasn't a fan of anyone in the Franklin family.

If Adam's adoptive mother, Helene, were a color, she'd be beige. All she really cared about anymore was her charity work, keeping her roots from showing, and not ending up in any of the tabloids. She hadn't always been like that, or so Adam had been told. Years with Franklin had made her into the kind of woman who kept quiet and looked pretty and ignored every bad act by her husband.

She'd been distantly kind to Adam, never motherly, but she'd never tried to cause him harm. For that, he would try not to cause her pain if it could be avoided.

"Helene hasn't had it easy either," Adam said, not wanting to cover this old ground again.

Justin shrugged, his expression morphing into

the closest thing Justin ever got to serious and Adam braced for what he knew was coming. It was a well-worn topic between them—as familiar as the focus on women, sex, money and poker was in their frequent late-night cigar-smoking sessions after long days making a company run. "It's not your job to take care of everyone, Adam. Redhawk/Ling isn't going to rise and fall on you alone."

"Justin, I know that but this is important. If we don't figure this out, I'm going to let a lot of people down. People who have banked their futures on Redhawk/Ling surviving."

"You mean 'we,' not 'I.'" Justin moved even closer to shove against his chest, his glare echoing the anger and frustration in his voice.

"I know," Adam replied, avoiding making direct eye contact. But Justin wasn't letting him off the hook that easily.

"No, I don't think you do." Justin grunted out the last of his frustration and scrubbed a hand against the stubble on his cheek. "Look, I'm done trying to change you but you've gotta start letting some of this shit go. Rely on other people. Now you've got a brother and sister to help you work on that life skill."

Oh yeah, the one subject sure to make him stress even more than usual. Now he had a family to worry about when he knew nothing about family.

"I'll be sure to call you out of your next weekend-long poker tournament to help out at the office. *That* will work," Adam grumbled, immediately feeling a pang of guilt at the jab that he knew would strike the soft underbelly of his oldest friend.

"Okay, now you're being an *asshole* and that's my cue to give you some space to brood and fixate on all the things you can't control." Justin paced over to the couch, grabbed his phone off the table and headed toward the door. "While you're pondering all the shit in the universe during your ninety-mile run tonight, don't forget to figure out what the hell was happening between you and Tess a little while ago."

And there it was. Payback for the poker comment. He deserved it.

"I'm not talking to you about that," he answered, not bothering to deny that he knew exactly what Justin was talking about.

He had to figure out how to navigate the fact that he'd called her *baby* and how hard it was to stay away from Tess. He'd failed miserably at not fantasizing about her or dreaming about her—why did he think that actual physical contact would be easier to navigate? There was no easy answer, but he had to make a decision to give in to temptation or cut Tess loose. And he knew in his gut that letting her go wasn't the answer.

"You were leaving, right?" Adam prompted, needing time to process the day's events.

"I was. I am. I'll be back here tomorrow morning and we'll find out who is trying to destroy our company." Justin pointed at him, his grin telling Adam that all was forgiven. "And we'll also discuss why you can't seem to understand the difference between asking Tess out and hiring her." He shook his head. "No wonder you're still single."

Four

"One day I'm going to show up and you'll be wearing an aluminum foil hat."

Tess put a Post-it on the file she was reviewing and looked up to find her baby sister leaning on the door frame swinging her set of house keys back and forth in front of her. Well, Mia wasn't a baby anymore. She was twenty-one years old, a junior in college and a testament to the fact that Tess had done something right.

Except for the part where Mia was such a smart-ass. That part was *all* Mia.

Okay, maybe that was all Tess.

"Is that how I taught you to speak to your elders?" Tess asked, surprised at the stiffness in her back and the tingly sensation running up and down one of her legs. She glanced down at her watch; she'd been head down for hours. She pushed back her desk chair and shook out her sleepy leg, smacking her sister's hand when she flipped open a file on the desk. "No peeking at stuff on my desk. I can't believe I still have to tell you this."

"I still can't believe that *you're* such a broken record," Mia grumbled, tapping her finger on the file in question. "I was just checking to see if this was about your favorite subject. I rang the bell twice and called out and you still didn't hear me."

Tess groaned, stretching out her leg as she headed toward the kitchen for the strongest, biggest cup of coffee on the planet. She still had a dozen files to read through before she could even think about hitting the sack. It had been a long week and it looked like it was about to get longer. Somebody was definitely trying to sabotage Redhawk/Ling and she'd been hired to do a job.

Adam was depending on her.

And she was lying to him.

Tess shook her head to clear the cobwebs and the memory of him and the way he'd called her *baby* in his office earlier. It had been unexpected and clearly, if the flare of surprise in his eyes was any indication, something he hadn't planned on saying. But the endearment had been uttered with a sexy rumble and a protective ferocity that sent a shiver of anticipation down her spine. Factor in how he'd been immediately concerned with the well-being of Estelle, his sweet assistant, and Tess added another item to the long list of reasons why she wanted to jump Adam Redhawk.

Okay, she really needed that caffeine.

"I was working, Mia. Why aren't you at school?" Tess shuffled behind the counter and flipped the switch on her coffee maker, grabbed a pod and slipped it into the machine. She turned around to lean on the countertop while the machine worked its magic and created the elixir that would keep her from making bad man-oriented decisions. "Not that I don't love seeing you but don't you have a paper to write or a class to attend? A study session with coeds in your pj's?"

"It's college, not an Anna Kendrick movie," Mia mumbled from where her head was stuck inside the fridge.

She emerged, her auburn pixie cut sticking up at odd angles due to the static electricity, a string cheese in her hand. For a minute, it was ten years ago and Mia was the pain-in-the-butt little sister who tried to listen in on Tess's phone calls with boys and who also crawled into bed with Tess when their father was having a rough spell. Those days solidified their relationship; they'd learned the hard way that in the end they really only had each other.

Tess had worked her ass off, juggling several jobs for a number of years and cases she would have loved to turn down to secure this little house. It was only two bedrooms and one bath and a backyard that was barely big enough for a grill but it was their home. Tess used the space in what was intended to be the dining room to work from home on the days she didn't need to go to the tiny office she leased from a local insurance company on a barter basis. She always kept Mia's room open for her and tried not to let on just how much she missed her since she'd gone to college.

"Fair enough but please don't join an a cappella group. That still doesn't explain why you're here." Tess held up a hand in defense at the site of her sister's glare. "Not that I don't love it when you come and see me but…"

Mia rolled her eyes and opened the string cheese. "I need to do my laundry."

"Of course, you do."

"*Whatever.* I also haven't heard from you in a couple of weeks and I wanted to make sure it was a case and not a serial killer home invasion that had removed you from your usual place of up my butt and all in my business."

Tess's machine gurgled and sputtered the signal that it was done and she turned to grab the mug of hot coffee. "I'm going to drink this and pretend that you're not here."

Mia sidled up beside her, chuckling as she nudged Tess to the side to start her own brew. "You love me and we both know it." Her sister nudged her again and leaned down to peek up at Tess. "Seriously though, are you okay? I haven't heard from you in a while."

Tess huffed out a sound that was part sigh and part laugh. "Define *okay*."

Mia frowned, tossing the cheese wrapper into the trash with a dunk shot that would have made their dad proud. Clearly, hours spent in the driveway shooting hoops had paid off. "Tess, I love you and I respect your dedication to the cause but you have got to let this vendetta go. Franklin Thornton is untouchable and always will be. He got away with it. End of story."

"No, that is not the end of the story," Tess fumed, sloshing coffee out of her mug when she picked it up with a little too much force.

"No, you're right. It's not the end of the story because the actual ending will read, 'Daughter ruins her life just like her father. Franklin Thornton wins twice.'" Mia emphasized her harsh words with a flourish of her hands in the air like she was highlighting a movie marquee. "Let it go, Tess. Get laid. Read a book. Go to a movie. Get a fucking life."

She didn't need the caffeine because her sister's words woke her up like an injection of epinephrine straight to the heart. Where fatigue and lethargy had weighed her down just moments before, she was now fueled by anger and a betrayal that cut to the quick.

"Fuck you, Mia." Tess squared off with her sister, her voice bouncing off the hardwood floors and cabinets. "If I don't have a life it's because I'm doing this for you and for Dad."

"Bullshit, Tess. I didn't ask you to do this and Dad has been dead for years and he doesn't care anymore. If you want to do something for me, then stop all this avenging angel crap and let me have some peace instead of carrying around all this guilt for everything you've done for me. If you can't let yourself off the hook, then get it off my back. Please."

Whoa. Tess blinked hard, trying to clear the roaring in her head and the hot tears stinging her eyes and blurring her vision. Mia's words pierced her deeply and Tess reached for her coffee, taking a too-hot sip to fill the heavy silence that polluted the air between them. It wasn't easy to hear that her efforts weren't recognized for what they were, that her sister didn't see the value in making the past right.

Mia had been so little—she didn't always remember just how bad it had been after Franklin Thornton had cheated their father and sent him spiraling into depression and self-destruction. But Tess remembered it all because she had been the one who had stepped in and shielded Mia from the worst of it. In a way, Tess had made it possible for Mia to not understand how she couldn't just let this go.

Tess wouldn't tell Mia that she'd met the man today, that he was as awful up close and personal as he was on paper and the internet. She wouldn't tell her because it wouldn't change anything for her sister. This was a conversation that they'd had in some form or other a million times before and she wasn't going to change her path so it was best to let it drop.

Tess cleared her throat, testing her voice a little before she changed the subject. "I wasn't working on the Thornton case, anyway. Adam Redhawk hired me to help him find someone."

"I thought you wrapped that case up," Mia said and Tess let out a grateful breath that she was going to let their fight over their dad and Franklin Thornton go.

"I did. This is a new one."

"That guy sure does lose a lot of people," Mia mused, her eyebrow raised in self-congratulatory amusement at her very bad joke.

"It's not that kind of case. Nobody is actually missing." Tess considered how much she could talk about and not violate her confidentiality agreement. "It's like a bunch of background checks on steroids."

"And he doesn't have anyone at that huge company he owns who could possibly do that for him? Not. At. All?" Mia shook her head on beat with her words, her grin wide and a little bit lascivious.

"Mia," Tess said, amused warning coating her response. She knew exactly where this was going and if it was possible, she wanted to talk about this topic even less than she wanted to argue over their father.

"Tess." Mia hopped up on the counter and kicked out to poke Tess with a purple sparkle–painted toe. "I saw you and Adam Redhawk together and let's just say that they can see the sparks zipping between you two from the space station. I felt like I needed to get you guys a room with a horizontal surface as soon as possible or risk the entire building going up in flames."

"I don't know what you're talking about." Tess shuffled over to the dishwasher, opening it to see if the load was clean and needed to be put away. She peered into the dim interior and found only a couple of plates and mugs on the racks; a clear reminder that she was a single woman living alone. She shut the door with a thud and desperately looked around the tidy space for anything that could distract her sister or at least give Tess a refuge from the turn this conversation was taking. She spied a stack of catalogs strewn across the coffee table in the family room that needed her immediate attention.

"The house is spotless, you neat freak. Stop avoiding the discussion," Mia yelled at her back from the kitchen.

"This isn't a discussion, it is you letting your imagination run on that little squirrel wheel in your head. Adam Redhawk and I have a professional relationship only. He had a job that needed discretion and I had done good work for him already and so he asked me to stay on. As a small business owner, I'm not going to turn down a good job."

Behind her she heard Mia jump down from the counter and she could feel the distance closing between them. Images of unsuspecting gazelles being stalked by cheetahs on the Nature Channel crossed her mind and Tess knew exactly who was the gazelle in this situation. She turned and faced her tenacious younger sister and decided to put this to rest once and for all.

Maybe she'd believe it herself this time.

"Mia, Adan Redhawk is a good guy..."

"And smokin' hot."

"Mia, please focus."

"I *did* focus. I focused on those pictures of him in the *L.A. Style* weekly the last time he competed in a triathlon. I focused on his six-pack and I focused on his biceps and I focused on his bounce-a-quarter-off-it ass. Believe me. I was *f-o-c-u-s-e-d.*"

Mia grinned as she sat on the arm of the sofa, grabbing Tess by the arm and dragging them both down onto the seat in a tumble of cushions, arms and legs. It brought back memories of the many nights they'd cuddled up like this together on shabbier furniture, heads bent together as they shared secrets. Tess missed those days when things had been simpler and her crush on a boy had been something she could indulge in. Before sex was a weapon and trust was a fiction.

"You're ridiculous," she murmured, wrapping a strand of her sister's hair around her finger. "Mia, I can't get involved with Adam."

"Because you might have to use him when you make your move to take down his father?" Mia asked, her expression ridiculously coy.

"Franklin Thornton *is not* Adam's father." Tess surprised herself at the visceral reaction Mia's words triggered in her gut. And her rapier tone shocked her sister as well, if the raised eyebrow and gaping mouth were any indication.

"Wow. Protective much?"

And that was exactly what she was feeling: protective. Protective of a man who'd had very little of that in his life but who offered it to so many people around him. His employees. His best friend. His long-lost siblings.

She was neck-deep in background files because he needed to protect Redhawk/Ling from an unknown enemy. He had stood toe-to-toe with Franklin, demanding an apology for Estelle, and had put his body between her and the man, physically trying to shield her from his words. Adam had come into her life because he needed to find his brother and sister, determined to ensure that they were okay.

Adam had a hero complex. In only the best way.

It wasn't the first time she wondered who protected Adam Redhawk. If he ever let anyone close enough to take care of him.

As far as she could tell, the answer to that question was a decided no.

"Yeah, I guess I am a little protective of him." Tess remembered the moment this afternoon in his office and the jolt of connection that had leaped between them and seared her skin and down deeper in a place she didn't want to acknowledge. "Franklin came into Redhawk/Ling today and Adam physically stepped in between the two of us. He actually used his body to shield me from the venom of Franklin Thornton." She paused, remembering the shiver-induced goose bumps that ran up and down her spine during the moments when they'd been so close and she'd had all of his focus on her. "It was intense."

"That's good. I'm glad. I think it's been a while since somebody looked out for you," Mia murmured, her voice low and tentative, as if she didn't want to scare Tess away from this conversation. "You must mean a lot to him."

Tess shook her head, confused about a lot of things but pretty clear on this situation. "Mia, he takes care of everybody. It's what he does. It's why his employees stick it out even if the risks they take at Redhawk/Ling aren't guaranteed. It's why he had me look for his brother and sister after so long. It was killing him not to know where they were or how they were doing. He is so confident in his ability to change the world that he couldn't imagine a world where he didn't find them and guarantee that they would never want for anything."

"And today he stood up for *you*."

"He did."

And he'd called her *baby*.

What would he call her when he learned about her deception? Not that she didn't have the best reason to walk that line between lie and truth. Franklin had irrevocably destroyed her family and she had to make him pay. Had to avenge her dad and restore his good name and reputation.

As much as Adam carried the burden of restoring his own family, he would understand why she had to do what she was doing.

They were really two sides of the same coin. Doing what they had to do to make things right for the people in their lives who mattered most.

At least that's what she'd tell herself every time Adam called her "baby."

Five

Adam was going to ignore the light on in Tess's office.

It was late at Redhawk/Ling. Not night-before-an-app-release late but there weren't many people in the building on this Tuesday night. All the ones who had lives had left long ago and Adam didn't want to dwell too long on what that meant about him and Tess. They'd been working from Robin Roberts to Conan O'Brian time with very little off-duty opportunity to do much but grab a run and hit the sheets. Alone.

Not that he hadn't thought about being in his king-size bed with somebody—somebody who looked a lot like Tess—but sleep deprivation and long hours hadn't diminished his belief that getting involved with the sexy redhead would be a very bad idea.

Tess was reading a file, taking notes on her laptop as she flipped between the pages. Her hair was piled on top of her head, curls sneaking loose and tumbling around her shoulders like a titian waterfall. Emerald green reading glasses were perched on her nose, the old-fashioned chain that helped her keep track of them looped around her neck. Dressed today in a black pinstriped double-breasted suit with high heels, she looked like his bossy librarian wet dream fantasy suddenly live and in person.

And it was ridiculously cliché and predictable but he barely resisted the compulsion to cover the distance between them and bend her over the desk—glasses intact—and explore every inch of her until this inconvenient and all-consuming need for her was nothing but embers and ash. Tess was driving him crazy, and in his sleep-deprived state he knew that being alone with her was a really bad life choice. What he wouldn't give to have just an iota of the poker-faced talent that Justin used at the card tables right now. Because he knew that nothing about his desire and need for Tess Lynch was hidden from anyone who was looking.

And Tess was looking. Whenever they were in each other's orbit it was as if their bodies and minds synced into perfect rhythm. They completed each other's sentences, reached for the same files at the same time, and jumped to the same conclusions. Justin said it was creepy but to Adam it was mesmerizing and enticing; for a man who'd been uprooted so early and had never found his balance it was the closest thing to equilibrium he had ever experienced. And Adam knew that it was dangerous in the best and worst ways as only the most visceral of need fulfillment could be.

He should leave; turn on his heels, walk down to his bike, go home and work out this insanity in the gym or in the bed of a woman who didn't make him want things he wouldn't do justice to.

But he knocked on Tess's door anyway.

"I order you to go home and do whatever it is you do when you're not working," he said, trying for an I-don't-really-care-what-you-do-when-you-go-home tone only to be undone when Tess lifted her head and smiled at him with a hazy focus that whispered of slow and easy mornings in bed. She was sexy as hell and his body thrummed in response, his dick getting hard under the well-worn denim of his jeans. Adam shifted slightly to try and hide his reaction.

Tess laughed, shaking her head as she leaned back in her chair and gave him the once-over. "I know you know me better than that. You don't really think that I'd allow anyone to 'order' me to do anything." She flashed him a grin and a raised eyebrow that said she had his number. "Even though I hear that you're really good at it."

Her words sucked all the oxygen out of the room, heat flashing like a wildfire along his skin as he struggled to catch his breath and steady his racing heart. Adam knew what she was referring to; he was discreet about his bedroom practices but he knew his partners were not and the stories about him were all true. Not that he kept a dungeon or anything in his basement but he often liked to be in control of the moment and his partner when he was having sex and it was in stark contrast to his usually reserved demeanor. It wasn't what people expected and that made it hot gossip in Silicon Valley.

Tess's grin faded and her cheeks flushed with a blush, something he'd never witnessed on her before. Her stammering would have been almost cute if he hadn't been so turned on.

"Adam, that was…holy hell, I can't believe I said that."

He waved off her apology as he moved into the office, feeling just how small it was with the sweet-hot tension building between them. He wasn't embarrassed by her comment—he was intrigued. Because Tess had sounded interested and that was something he had no choice but to explore.

"Well, I *am* really good at it." Adam kept his eyes locked on hers as he rounded her desk, stopping just shy of her personal space but close enough to feel the heat generated by their proximity and chemistry. Pure chemical reaction. Spontaneous combustion.

He crossed his arms over his chest as he leaned against the edge of her desk, his last-ditch effort to keep his hands off Tess Lynch. Adam locked on her gaze, now defiant and smoldering with any hint of embarrassment long gone. His stare flicked away long enough to note the white-knuckle grip she maintained on the arms of her chair, a welcome reminder that he wasn't the only one struggling with what was brewing between them.

He ended the standoff. It was time.

"I'm a decisive man, Tess."

"Yes. I am aware." She rose from the chair and he tracked her movements, soaking in the way she moved in closer, but not close enough to touch. With her heels on, they were almost eye to eye, mouth to mouth, chest to breast. "You are also private, loyal, harsh, fair and intense." Her voice lowered and he leaned in closer to catch every word. "And you're very sexy."

Adam let his gaze drop to her mouth, giving himself one last chance to not do the thing that would complicate an already complicated situation. His gaze traveled higher and he locked eyes with Tess, the arching of her right brow in question and invitation cutting through the last, fragile threads of his common sense.

Her mouth was soft, lips warm, and she tasted like the sweetest fruit: like all things forbidden. Tess took a moment to react, her breath caught on a swift intake of surprise that quickly gave way to her leaning into the kiss and opening to his tongue. Her fingers ghosted over his chest, his hands skimming over her arms and along the curve of her hips, their only firm connection the warm, wet tangle of their tongues and the hungry press of their lips.

Adam ended it first, needing to attempt a small grip on his sanity. "Damn. Tess, that—"

With that one sexy eyebrow raised again and a grin teasing at her swollen lips, Tess skated her hand down his torso, letting it hover over his aching hard-on. "If you say it was a mistake and apologize, you'll regret it."

If Adam didn't think that he could be in serious trouble with this woman, that moment sealed it. Smart and ballsy, Tess was a puzzle he was compelled to decipher, an indulgence that he would allow himself for once. For tonight.

"I'll never regret that kiss. The question is what we do next." Adam snaked his hands around her waist, pulling her lush body against his for the first time outside of his fantasies. Tess fit against him perfectly, her full breasts pressing against his chest, her long legs entwined with his, her hips cradling his hard length with heat that tempted him to strip her down and move on from kisses to something more. "I'll make it clear what I want."

"I'll add that you are direct to that list of things I know about you," Tess said, her fingers warm against his chest, her hips bucking against his own as she gave him a mischievous smirk. "But I think I know what you want."

Adam chuckled, his grip tightening on her hips

to keep her from moving. If she kept that up, he'd bend her over the desk and make a mess of her and the files strewn across the surface. But he had somewhere to go and something to do.

He leaned in and pressed a kiss against her temple, groaning again when she wiggled against him. "I just want to be clear because we are working together. It could get complicated."

"Adam, it won't get complicated," Tess said with conviction as she unwound herself from his grip, her hands moving to fix her hair and straighten her suit as she rounded to the other side of the desk. He wanted to pull her back into his arms but this was a conversation they probably needed to have with some acreage between them. "You don't do complicated. You do sex. Great sex. You do clear rules and parameters with your bed partners and nothing that lasts over a couple of months. They don't leave happy but they do leave knowing that you were honest with them."

Tess held her hands out in a "how did I do?" gesture and Adam let out a harsh breath of shock. He wasn't sure why he was surprised at her information. He'd hired her because she was good at what she did and his sex life wasn't something he spoke about but it wasn't a secret in the small community of Silicon Valley. In the end, it was relief that settled low in his belly, relief that whatever they decided tonight, they would be on the same page.

But he didn't have to have a full dossier on her to understand her.

"I could say the same thing about you, Tess. No long-term relationships for you. No strings." When she raised an eyebrow and put her hand on her cocked hip, he bit back a laugh. Bull's-eye for him. Adam strode around the desk, moving slowly toward the very kissable and very tempting woman he desperately hoped would accept what he could offer. "So, are we on? No strings? Nothing serious? I have enough serious in my life. Hundreds of employees that depend on me and a new family that I have no clue how to navigate."

"And when the job is over?"

He nodded, reaching out to wrap an arm around her waist to pull her close. "When the job is over, it's over. Can you live with that, Tess Lynch?"

Tess stared at him, her green-gold eyes shrewd but lit with heat that gave away what her answer was going to be. She wasn't a woman to back down from what she desired and she wanted him as much as he wanted her.

"I can live with that, Adam Redhawk."

Adam laughed, leaning in to brush a swift kiss against her mouth before checking his watch.

Tess glared, glancing down at his watch. "Do you have somewhere to be?"

"Yeah." Until tonight, he'd never regretted his second Tuesday of the month plans in his life. But he didn't want to let Tess go. Not yet. She was clearly up for propositions tonight and maybe she'd go for another. "Have you ever been a groupie?"

Six

Tess added "owning a motorcycle" to her bucket list.

She loved the hum of an engine and hot metal in between her legs as she sped down the road with nothing between her and high-speed danger. It was a thrill that couldn't be rivaled by many things. Sex, great sex, was one of those things but the instances of *that* kind of sex she'd had in her lifetime didn't outnumber the fingers on her right hand.

The hand currently settled over Adam's heart and gripping his tight, black T-shirt as they sped down the road, chasing the city lights and dodging cars filled with people looking for a good time. Tess took advantage of the ride requiring her to hold on tight to the hard-bodied man nestled between her legs, and indulged in the anticipation of this night and their new arrangement.

Adam's black Heritage Classic Harley-Davidson was a sweet ride, powerful and loud and everything you wanted a motorcycle to be. It was an odd choice for such a quiet man who did nothing to grab for attention. But it suited him when you really got to know him.

This bike was outward evidence of the part of Adam he buried down deep inside of him: reckless, intense and rebellious. Adam was a man of a million layers and she wanted to unpeel every single one.

So, it was a no-brainer to change her clothes and jump on the back of his bike to find out what the hell he did the second Tuesday of every month. Tess knew where he went, she'd discovered it during her background check of him, but something had held her back from following him inside the bar located on the seedier side of the Valley and finding out exactly what it was that brought him there every month, come rain or come shine.

Before she knew it and before she wanted the ride to end, they pulled up in front of Duke's, passing by the entrance to enter a parking lot and head to an empty space. Duke's had seen better days, the front of the building a dirty brick and the sign faded, but it had a loyal clientele and was packed almost every night. Live music and a generous pour were the hallmarks of this local institution.

Adam motioned to a guy sitting in a booth in the parking lot, giving him a thumbs-up of thanks and acknowledgment when the guy waved him in. Adam cut the engine, slipped off his helmet and twisted to look at Tess. She bit back a grin, unwilling to let him see just how adorably sexy he was with his dark hair mussed and an excited smile on his face. He reached into a side bag and pulled out a black baseball cap with Stanford embroidered on it, placing it low on his head so that the bill hid part of his face.

"You ready?" he asked, turning and reaching up to help her remove her helmet. His grin was genuine, a little bit shy and all kinds of sexy. "I'm running a little late."

"A little late for what? You never did tell me exactly what is happening here." Tess watched him hop off the seat and she accepted his outstretched hand to help her do the same. She'd changed into a jade-green T-shirt-style mini-dress and ankle boots and the length of her skirt required her to maneuver a bit to not land on her face on the pavement or flash the patrons of Duke's milling about the parking lot.

Adam held on to her hand, lacing their fingers together, his eyes mischievous but narrowed a bit with skepticism. "Are you telling me that you *really* don't know why I come here?"

She shook her head, allowing him to tug her along

to a side entrance as she waited for him to clue her in. "It wasn't necessary for the job."

Adam paused at the door. "That never stopped you before."

She shrugged, opting to go for honesty on this one, even if it was embarrassing. "I wanted to leave some things for you to tell me."

Her reward for her candor was a quick, hard kiss and a flash of his dimple before he pulled the door open and she was hit by a wall of sound from the crowd of people inside Duke's. The space was dim but not dark, the long bar visible where it ran the length of the room on one side. There was a stage at the end of the room and on it a band was setting up for the show. As if on cue, the two men and one woman on stage turned and waved at Adam.

It was too noisy to hear what they were saying but their gestures were the universal symbol for "where the fuck have you been?" and suddenly Tess had a pretty good idea about what Adam did here once a month on the second Tuesday.

Adam turned back to her, gesturing toward the stage. "I've got a tab here. Order whatever you want and there's a table up front for our guests."

Tess gripped his arm, tugging him back to get a little more info. "Whose guests? Who are those people?"

Adam grinned, his smile contagious and de-aging him about a decade. Tess caught her breath, grateful to have saved this revelation for now, this time and this place. He was so damn cute, sexy, so excessively fuckable. Agreeing to indulge in this thing between them was looking like one of the best mistakes she ever made. Now she only wondered how long this gig would go before she and Adam could get back to one of their places and a horizontal surface.

"It's my band, The Double E's!"

"Your *what*?"

"My band." He winked at her. "Didn't you ever wonder why I have drumsticks all over my office?"

Tess had wondered but had figured that they were his version of those fidget widgets, something for him to mess with as he let his mind solve all the problems at Redhawk/Ling. And even though she'd purposefully left some things in his life unrevealed, once again Adam Redhawk had surprised her more than she'd considered possible. The drumsticks constantly lying around in his office weren't props.

It looked like Adam Redhawk was a secret rock star. Sweet Lord, this was a sexy tidbit she really didn't need to know.

"Why the Double E's?" she asked, tugging on his arm as he moved to head to the stage.

"We started playing together at Stanford. It seemed like a good name for a bunch of electrical engineering majors."

She watched him stride across the room with palpable excitement, and up onto the stage where he traded high fives and back slaps with the very-average-looking-not-a-rock-star-among-them group. They looked like a group of electrical engineers. Engineers who played in a rock band the second Tuesday of every month.

Adam eased behind the drum kit, reaching down to grab a set of sticks and twirling them between his fingers. Tess laughed, startled by the tap on her shoulder.

"I *knew* I should have bet on it." Justin Ling was smiling, waggling his eyebrows up and down like the idiot he pretended he was. "I would have cleaned up."

Tess wasn't fooled by his usual court jester act but she was thirsty. "I have no idea what that means but I know you don't need the money from that bet to buy me a drink."

"True enough. But let me get one for you. I'm just going to put it on Adam's tab anyway," Justin answered with a grin, motioning for her to follow him over to the bar. He was slim, tall with an athletic build and possessed a presence that made the crowd part like the Red Sea. Once more she was thrown by the difference between Adam and Justin: one made every effort to fade into the shadows and the other was disappointed if the spotlight wasn't bright enough.

It was starting to get crowded; what looked like students piling in to fill the bar, all yelling drink orders and staking out claims to tables. It wasn't a dive but it wasn't a trendy Silicon Valley bar either. This had more of a local vibe; a neighborhood place where regular people came to meet friends and hook up. And from the snippets of conversations she was picking up, they were excited to see the band.

Justin traded high-fives with the bartender and shouted their order, only waiting a minute to have their drinks served. He grabbed the two bottles, nodding toward a table in front of the stage marked with a reserved sign on it. They settled on the stools, both taking sips of their beer as they watched the band warm up.

"Thanks for the drink." Tess saluted Justin across the table. "Now tell me more about this bet you didn't take."

He waggled his finger at her. "I'm not sure I should tell you. That might be breaking the 'wingman code.'"

"What the hell is the 'wingman code'?" Tess asked, glancing over when the band started a short sound check. "They aren't bad."

Justin threw a look over his shoulder at them and shrugged. "They don't suck."

"And you're his best friend? High praise." Tess poked him in the arm to get his attention back to answering her question. "What is the 'wingman code'?"

"It means that I shouldn't tell you that I *almost* bet Adam that he would eventually bring you here. You see, if I told you that I told him he was interested in you as more than an independent contractor *and* that I told him he would bring you here to try to impress you…well, *that* would be breaking the 'wingman code.'" Justin saluted her with his drink and grinned from ear to ear. "But I wouldn't do that."

"Of course not." Tess laughed at him, shaking her head at his absurdity. Justin Ling was the very loose yin to Adam's tightly wound yang and it was easy to see why they were such good friends and even better business partners.

"Do you like him?" Justin surprised her with his question and shocked her even more with his attempt to look like it didn't matter. But it clearly did matter and it should when you were just trying to look out for your best friend. It was sweet and it deserved a straight answer, so she gave him the most honest one she could.

"I do like him." She swirled her finger in the condensation formed on the glass of the beer bottle, mulling over how much she wanted to share about her situation with Adam. She couldn't try to convince Justin that there was nothing going on; he'd never believe it. "But this isn't anything to get excited about. It has a shelf life."

Justin leveled a look at her that gave away nothing. No surprise that he was so successful at the poker table. "That's a real shame, Tess. Total bullshit but also a real shame."

She sputtered and spilled beer on the table, preparing to argue with him about the bullshit comment but the band started playing a really loud song and any chance for argument was lost. Tess glared at him, noted that Justin was no longer paying any attention to her, and then focused on the happenings on the stage.

The band was tight, with a driving sound and excellent vocalist, but they really lacked stage presence. Not one of them really engaged with the audience, even though the crowd was completely riveted on them. Her attention was riveted on Adam.

Adam was seated behind the drum kit, baseball cap pulled down low over his face while he wailed away in a rhythm guaranteed to get people on their feet. And it was working. The crowd was dancing, the energy enough to raise the roof, and Adam looked sexy-as-hell with his arm muscles flexing with every beat.

Tess couldn't take her eyes off him. Adam was a commanding man, quietly owning a room with his brilliant mind and determined focus but this was a wholly new outlet for all of that intensity. One song ran into the next, and the crowd got bigger and rowdier with every one.

And then the set was over and she was on her feet cheering for the band as they took their bows. Without any fanfare, Adam jumped down from the stage and bounded over to her, sweaty and boyishly sexy with the baseball cap now turned backward. His grin was wide and contagious and she offered no resistance when he pulled her against him with a hand around her waist and took her mouth in a kiss.

They broke apart, still laughing, and he looked down at the table and grabbed her beer, chugging down half of it in a few long swallows.

"Hey! That's my drink," she protested, shoving against his chest. "Is this how you treat a groupie, rock star?"

"If you were any good at being a groupie, you'd have my own cold beer waiting for me."

"Well, if you were Mick Jagger, I would."

"Ha! I knew I liked her," Justin interjected, handing off a beer to both of them as he returned from the bar. "She won't take any of your shit and she's completely unimpressed by this 'I'm in a rock band' crap."

"You're just jealous," Adam shot back.

"Well, of course I am," Justin said with a comical roll of his eyes. "Women love rock stars."

Adam waved him off, looking down at her with curiosity. "So, what did you think?"

"I think I'm pissed that I didn't come to hear you sooner. You guys are really good." Tess ran her hand over his chest, ending with a poke in his side. "And it really explains all of the drumsticks lying around your office."

Adam grinned at her, his gaze slipping down to

her mouth, and her heart pounded, her mouth going dry at the heat in his intense focus. Tess wasn't one to hesitate once she'd made up her mind and she'd made up her mind about this fling with Adam.

He was smiling when their lips met, the pressure soft and teasing. Tess ran her tongue along his bottom lip and she felt rather than heard his groan at the touch. Adam tugged her around to face him, his large hands on her hips as he pulled them flush against each other. He slanted his mouth over hers, tongue now invading as he deepened the connection between them.

The noise around them faded into a blur of music and voices as they sank into each other. He tasted of beer and heat and the promise of something darker. Her hands wandered over his chest, the softness of the T-shirt fabric covering the hard muscles underneath. Tess was dying to lift his shirt and find out what was hiding under the clothes but this was not the place, although they had decided that it was their time.

Adam broke the kiss, his hands lifting to frame her face, fingers tangling in her hair. "I've got something I want to show you."

"I'm pretty sure I want to see it," she answered, allowing the leer to coat every word.

Adam took a step back and held out his hand, the dimple showing when she slipped her hand in it. "Well, then, let's go."

Seven

"This is *not* what I expected you to show me."

Adam hooked the helmets on the back of the bike, turning to watch Tess as she paced the length of the long patio behind the Lick Observatory. It was clear tonight, the stars brilliant against the dark sky, so bright that you didn't even need the huge telescope housed in the observatory building just to the right of where they stood to see them.

"Well, one of us needs to get their mind out of the gutter," he said, sputtering out a laugh when she whirled around, green eyes wide and hands on her hips in indignation.

"Oh really?" Tess sauntered toward him, her

stride half dangerous swagger and half sensual invitation. "If you haven't noticed, this place is closed. Are the cops going to show up and arrest us for trespassing?"

Now it was his time to swagger, and it was easy when being with Tess made him feel ten feet tall. He moved toward her, meeting her in the middle of the patio, reaching out to pull her flush against him. Adam loved her curves, her breasts, hips and ass reminiscent of the pin-up girls of the 1940s. But what made her absolutely mouthwatering was the way she owned her body, the utter confidence she had in her power as a woman.

Women in his family's wealthy circles lived as though their money or connections gave them what Tess had naturally. They hid behind designer labels and expensive vacations that were handed over to them on a platter and never had to fight or scrape for their place in this world.

But Tess was a self-made woman, independent and strong, and he didn't even have to know all of her story to know that she'd had a rough time of it. She was everything he wanted and even more than he was sure he could handle.

But he'd be damned if he wouldn't give it his best try.

"We don't have to worry about the cops."

"Sure about that?" Tess asked, running her hands up his chest and over his shoulders, her fingers tangling in his hair. Her touch was electric, lighting him up from the inside out, brighter than any star in the sky.

"I'm as sure as a half-million-dollar donation to the observatory foundation last year."

"And I thought my twenty-five-dollar donation to the fire department was living large."

"Did I tell you that this is one of my favorite places?" Adam asked, taking her hand and leading her over the stone wall running along the edge of the overlook that led to the wooded valley below. He stood behind her, one arm wrapped around her waist and the other gesturing toward the broad swath of sky surrounding them.

"I used to come here and stare at the stars. We came here on a field trip in school and I fell in love with the way this sits so high above everything. It reminded me of the mountains where I lived when I was little and how you could hike to the top of the ridge and the stars seemed like they were so close you could reach out and touch them." He pointed to a different area as he named each constellation in turn. "The Big and Little Dipper. Orion's Belt. The North Star. I could come here and I knew that the stars I saw here were shining down on my family… wherever they were." Adam kissed her neck, noticing her little shiver at his touch and ramping back his surge of anticipation. Tess was here and there was no hurry. He buried his face in the soft fall of her hair, pressing kisses and tiny love bites over the exposed skin of her throat. "Pretty sappy, I know."

"Not sappy," she replied, nuzzling back. "Have you talked to your brother and sister?"

He nodded, resting his chin on her shoulder and his cheek against the silk of her hair as he recalled the phone calls it had taken him three hours of psyching himself up to make.

"Yeah. Roan was cool, running off to some gallery thing so he couldn't talk long. We set up another time later this week." Adam had been relieved to hear the genuine interest in his brother's voice. "He sounded really glad to hear from me."

"And Sarina?" Tess asked, the tentative edge to her voice betraying her worry.

"Sarina wasn't an easy call." He sighed, voicing the concerns that had almost kept him from hiring Tess to find his siblings. "When I first started looking for them, I was worried that they were dead, that I was too late. But, since I heard that you found them, I've been up nights worried that they wouldn't want anything to do with me."

Tess's fingers wove together with his own, a squeeze that let him know he wasn't alone. "Did Sarina say that to you?"

"No. No." Adam replayed the very brief phone call with his sister. "She was just…flat. I've had more interest from Siri."

"Keep trying. Sarina has had a hard life, built

ways to protect herself." Tess leaned back and pressed a kiss to his jaw. "She's worth the extra work."

"Have you met me? I'm never giving up on her. She's my sister." He paused, wondering how they'd swerved onto this topic. This wasn't what he'd had planned and it wasn't a place he wanted to be right now. Not when he had Tess in his arms under the stars. "Sorry. Pretty sappy."

"You're not sappy," she repeated, her ass pressing against his rapidly hardening dick. "Pretty sweet and crazy sexy."

"Sexier than being a rock star?" he teased, ghosting a kiss over her lips and relieved to be back on track for tonight's planned events.

Tess chuckled at that, the laugh evolving into a moan as his lips grazed her earlobe and his hand traveled up her stomach, cupping her breast at its final destination. Her nipple was hard, jutting against the soft material of her dress, and he could not resist rubbing the pad of his thumb over it, softly pinching it and grinding his erection against her when she gasped and dug her fingernails into his thighs. The pinch of pain was electric, sending the aftershock of pleasure racing along his nerve endings, emphasizing every rub of his own hard nipples against the softness of his T-shirt, the press of his zipper against his long, stiff length.

This moment was the manifestation of a fantasy

he'd lived on for months. His need for Tess had been there since the first meeting and he'd worked so hard not to give in and so had she; both were aware of the high-tension wire attraction that sizzled and snapped between them at every interaction. And here they were, on the verge of a moment that would destroy all of the carefully created walls that kept them apart for very good reasons. And while they'd agreed earlier, agreed to set everything on fire and contain the blaze, he wanted to be sure. They needed to be sure.

"Tess, I've got to know if this is still what you want," he growled against the curve of her jaw, surrounded by the sweet scent of her citrus perfume and the arousal-fueled aroma of her skin. She was writhing against him, falling with him into the enticing bliss of their pleasure, and he needed to hear her say yes just one more time before he let them both fall over the edge. "We can stop if you want to. No repercussions, no fallout."

Tess turned in his arms, backing up against the stone half wall as she met his gaze head-on. Her eyes were sharp with their intensity, clear even in the midst of the haze of sex they were currently stirring to life between them. He watched in fascination as she inched up the miniscule skirt of her dress, each tangle of her fingers in the fabric exposing another sliver of the soft pale skin of her thighs.

Her panties were black, a lace pattern that covered the place he longed to touch and taste, and with slow, deliberate movements they were sliding down her long legs and then lying in a puddle on the patio. Tess's curls were dark red and neatly trimmed; his attention was riveted there for a few moments by the sensual weaving of her fingers in their springy tangle. He forced his gaze to return to her face, needing to see that she was one hundred percent in this with him. If she backed out, it wouldn't be the first time he'd gone home horny and hungry for Tess; it hadn't impacted their working relationship in the past and if the brakes went on now, it wouldn't be a problem in the future.

Tess's voice was clear. "Adam, I know what I want and it is you. Like we agreed—no strings and we both walk away when we're done."

Adam took two steps forward, taking her mouth and inhaling her words as if they were the very life force he needed to keep breathing from one minute to the next. Tess opened to him immediately, her surrender echoing his own demand, and the heat between them rose with every rub of tongue and slide of lips.

She wasn't sweet, but Tess's brand of need was addictive and he already knew he'd have to tread carefully on this path or he'd find himself on the wrong side of what this was supposed to be about. He didn't have time for a relationship and he really didn't have time to be nursing a yearning for a woman he couldn't have.

Adam leaned her against the half wall, pressing kisses along her jawline, and down the pale column of her throat. The V-neck of her dress allowed him access to the delicate line of her collarbone and the shadowy top of the sweet cleft between her breasts, and he tasted, licked, nipped as much as he could reach. Tess writhed against him, bracing herself against the edge of the wall as she wrapped her legs around his waist.

Adam slid his hands down her body, cupping her bare ass and lifting her up in the air so that he bore all of her weight. From this position, Tess gazed down at him and he could see every detail of her expression. He observed the way her lids fluttered halfway closed when he grazed the folds of her sex. Observed the way she tried to bite back her moan when he found her slick and hot and spread it over her clit. Groaned out his own desire when he dipped a finger inside her heat and she lifted herself up and down on the digit, taking her own pleasure. He was absolutely at her service.

"Jesus, Tess, you feel better than I dreamed. Go ahead, take what you need, baby."

He used his thumb to massage her clit, adding another finger as she anchored her hands on his shoulders, grinding down on his fingers. Adam loved this look on Tess, debauched and hungry, powerful and honest. She leaned down, claiming his mouth in a fierce kiss of teeth and tongues, tasting of the months they denied themselves the sating of this primal need.

They broke off the kiss, Tess's cheeks flushed and her lips swollen and red. She threw her head back, her passion-coated shout of laughter ringing out into the night.

"You look like a queen with the stars making up your crown," he whispered, letting the awe in his voice shine through. "And every true sovereign deserves to be worshipped."

Adam slid her down his body, ending with her sitting on the half wall. He dropped to his knees at her feet, running his hands along her inner thighs, pushing the hem of her dress to expose the soft curls hidden beneath. He took his time, tracing the blue veins lying just under the skin, following with soft kisses and tender nips that made her gasp.

"I've never known anyone like you, Adam Redhawk," she whispered, her nails digging into his shoulders in an attempt to drag him closer. He resisted with a smile; he was going to take his time.

"Well, that just means that you never had a man who appreciated what an incredible woman you are." He placed a kiss next to her right knee. "Stupid men not knowing what they had." A kiss on the left leg. "You're smart." A lick on the right inner thigh. "Beautiful." A bite on a tender spot on the left. "Strong." Another kiss. "Powerful." Another lick. "Sexy as hell."

"Lean back," he said, watching as she leaned back slowly until she was resting on her elbows, looking down at him with eyes heavy lidded and dark with her desire. Her breasts rose and fell rapidly, her chest expanding with each ragged, panting breath.

"Tess, you are so damn perfect," he confessed, his own heart beating like the rhythm he'd pounded out on the drum kit earlier in the evening. He leaned forward, taking the first long, thirsty look at her sex in the full moonlight.

With his hands trembling with excitement, Adam ran his thumbs over her lips, making sure to give special attention to the places that made her gasp and squirm. He didn't want this to end too soon, needed to take his time to savor every second since he'd been dreaming of it for so long. So, he kept it slow, light, a gentle graze along the flesh designed to awaken every nerve and every pleasure.

Slick and wet, he couldn't wait any longer to taste what was on offer. He slid his hands under her thighs, under the sweet, round globes of her ass and lifted her, gently tugging her toward the edge of the half wall. Tess was level with his mouth, her sexy, sweet body just waiting for his touch, and he wavered between teasing her a little longer or indulging the pleasure he craved. He was hard, throbbing in his jeans, but he pushed it to the back of his mind. His only thought was doing everything he could to make Tess come apart.

Her first taste was heaven, so sweet and edged with the spice of her need. It was a first kiss, a first taste, his first step toward total addiction. Adam lapped at her, long licks, slow kisses, all calculated to push her over the edge. Tess's hands roamed over his shoulder, nails digging into his muscles and then traveling upward to tangle in his hair. He let her guide him, reading her pulls and presses and letting her control where she wanted his touch as he drove her desire higher and higher.

Adam watched her face when he finally—finally—grazed her clit. Tess moaned and grasped his hair tighter in her fist as she thrust her hips forward, greedy and begging. Delicious. It wouldn't take much more to get her to the end but he wanted to stretch it out a little while longer. A trip to heaven shouldn't be over too soon. Tess was very wet, so his finger slid into her easily, her body tight and hot on his skin. She cried out again, loud enough for it to echo in the ravine and Adam angled his tongue against her bundle of nerves, willing to do anything to hear that sound again.

Gently, he pressed his finger deeper inside, thrusting it slowly in and out, adding a second when she pressed down hard against it, seeking more and more friction, more sensual invasion. Tess rode his hand, her nails now grazing his scalp, and the pinpricks of pain shot straight to his cock, bringing him to the very point of the intersection of pain and pleasure.

Tess was writhing against his face, one of her hands now running over her breasts, her belly, fingers pinching the hard, tight peaks of her nipples through the fabric of her dress. Her eyes were closed tightly, lips parted on every sigh and pant of breath. She was a feast for his eyes and mouth and he rewarded her with intense focus on her clit.

Tess trembled, her thighs clenching around his head as frustrated and desperate moans passed over her lips. Her orgasm was *right there*, and he could not wait to see her fall apart around him, on him. With an addition of a third finger, Tess seized up, her body frozen as her pleasure hit her like a star shooting across the sky.

Adam rode out the pleasure with her, continuing to lick and suck and kiss her flesh until she pushed him away, her body limp and boneless above him. He rose up over her, kissing along her jaw and neck, claiming her mouth in a sweet tangle of lips and tongues as she came back down to earth.

Tess rose up, sliding to the ground in front of him on her knees. Her eyes were open as their tongues slid against each other, her hands trailing down his chest, fingers fumbling to undo his jeans. He broke off the kiss with a moan that rattled up from his gut when her fingers wrapped around his shaft. Her first touch was tentative, exploratory, her fingers tightening around him when he thrust up into her grip.

He groaned and Tess smiled, causing a shiver of

lust to race through him. She stroked him, her grip firm and hot and slicker with each pass. It was hot, sexy as hell, but the connection that kept his eyes locked on hers was visceral, elemental. He moved against her, snapping his hips up into her grip in a rhythm calculated to drive him closer and closer to the endgame.

"Come on, Adam. I'm your queen. I demand it."

Her tone was all it took. He was already on edge, tuned up to one hundred times his usual level of endurance. The tingling started in his spine, racing through his veins and under his skin and then spilling out of him with a shout and a deep, greedy kiss.

Long moments stretched into minutes as they leaned against each other, heartbeats slowing down to a normal pace, sweat cooling on their skin in the chilly evening air. Adam leaned back against the half wall, pulling Tess against him and tucking her against his chest as they both looked up at the stars.

The silence wasn't awkward, sex hadn't changed that between them, and Adam breathed out a sigh of relief. He'd wanted Tess but he'd wanted her body and her mind and the way he and she worked together, the way they'd moved in sync. This way when their affair was over, they could still be friends, still be in each other's lives. That prospect made the sex even sweeter, hotter.

"That was amazing, Tess," he murmured, brushing a kiss against her temple.

"Of course it was," she murmured. "It's why we avoided it for so long."

Adam felt the truth of that statement, knowing in his gut that was why he'd steered clear of giving in to his obsession with Tess until now.

Lights moved on the long drive that led to the observatory and they both sat up a little straighter. It could be another pair of lovers ready to do some stargazing of their own or it could be the police. Either way, it was time for them to leave. Adam rose to his feet, helping Tess as they searched for her underwear in the shadows. Laughing, they snatched them up from the ground and Tess shoved them in her pocket.

"How much did you say your donation was again?" Tess asked as they strode over to the bike, grabbed the helmets on the back and slipped them on. "Enough to get us out of this?"

Adam glanced quickly at the approaching car. "Let's not stay around to find out. Run for it?"

"Like Bonnie and Clyde?"

Adam considered this option, willing to go with it…to a point. "As long as it's the version with more sex and no murders or bank robberies, I'm in."

Tess jumped onto the bike, blowing him a kiss. "Well, hop on, Clyde. Let's go chase some stars."

It was the best offer he'd had in a very long time.

Eight

"A woman cannot live by takeout Chinese alone," Tess declared as she dug into her Szechuan chicken with a pair of chopsticks.

The food was delicious, delivered hot and fresh from her favorite restaurant, and normally she would have loved it except that tonight was the most recent of too many nights eating out of cartons or pizza boxes in the offices of Redhawk/Ling, trying to find the mole. They were racing against the clock and Adam and Justin and Tess were killing themselves to win that race. Adam and Justin had the business to run so most of the time it was just Tess and the IT guys they'd put at her disposal. Tonight, Justin had a family thing to attend so it was Tess and Adam in his office digging over piles and piles of information.

And the piles of information—physical and digital—kept growing. Tess was skilled at searching databases and sites to uncover people and their secrets but the volume that had to be processed during this short time was more than one person could tackle. So, the gift of the IT guys meant more eyes on more data and a quicker elimination of dead leads and people who could not be their mole. The last piece of the puzzle was out there, she just needed to find it.

"We could always order something different," Adam offered from his place at the table across from her, his carton of shrimp with pea pods in brown sauce sitting by his stack of documents. He cocked his head to one side, observing her, a slow grin taking over his face and showing off the dimple that made her want to kiss it and then him—all over. He picked up his food, scooping up chopstickfuls to eat. "Or we could always go out."

It was past midnight and the building was dark, empty except for the two of them and the guards settled in down at the entrance. She was exhausted and so was Adam, the dark circles under his eyes testifying to how little sleep he'd been getting these days. But Tess couldn't claim being the cause of his fatigue. They'd yet to spend an entire night together, opting to have sex at the office or in a car. But the encounter always saw them sated and separately in their own beds at the end of the night.

Though they couldn't keep away from each other, neither of them wanted to take this fling to their homes, content to exist in this half state in between work and their personal lives where nothing mattered except that they wanted each other. Tess squirmed in her seat, her body still aching a little from the last time they'd been together—hot and fast on her desk in her office. It had been fun, the need to be quiet only ramping up the pleasure and making it hotter.

But they'd never suggested adding any activity other than sex to their time together.

"Go out?" She knew what he meant but she was stalling for time, trying to figure out how she felt about his suggestion. Did she *want* to take this out of the shadows?

Hell. It didn't matter what she wanted. No strings. Nothing serious. Adding anything that resembled dating was something she should not do. It was something she might not be able to live with later.

As long as it was just sex she was comfortable walking in the gray area of her real reason for staying close to Adam. He got her one step closer to Franklin and avenging her father.

And *that* was why she was here. Not to date Adam Redhawk. Not to fall for Adam Redhawk.

It didn't matter that she wanted him. That she

liked him. None of that mattered, even if she wanted it to.

Adam nodded, still picking at his food. His movements were jerky, nervous, but he plowed ahead anyway. "Yeah, like a date."

"Ummm…this had a shelf life…we agreed."

"And having a meal together in an actual restaurant and not surrounded by a stack of papers covered with ridiculously private information about my employees is a deal breaker?" he asked, giving her an innocent look banked in an otherwise unreadable expression.

She couldn't tell if he was kidding or not but if she couldn't be honest about the real reason she was here, she could be honest about the sexual relationship between them.

"It might be. I think it should be."

"I'm not talking about what it *should* be," he answered. "I'm talking about what we want, which I think is really all that matters." Adam set his carton down, grabbed his beer from the table and took a sip. "And I'm not asking for us to go steady or to even change our Facebook status. I just thought we could have a meal at a restaurant before we do wicked things to each other."

Tess shook her head, letting her laugh bubble past her lips as she put down the carton and reached for a spring roll. Now *she* was stalling, attempting to parse through the butterflies doing somersaults in her stomach. But one sensation came through loud and clear: she wanted to go to that restaurant with him. Adam was the real deal. A good man, smart and ambitious and so incredibly determined. When he set his sights on you—when he set them on her—she felt like she was the only woman in the world, like she mattered beyond taking care of other people and righting old wrongs. It felt like she might matter to someone, to him, just because she made him happy. And that was a feeling no one had ever given her.

Damn. This was getting complicated. Sex she could handle. Amazing, off-the-charts sex, leaving-her-limp-and-wrung-out sex, ruin-her-for-other-men sex; she could handle all of that but this was new territory. Scary. Enticing. Not a good idea at all.

But she still couldn't say no.

"Can I think about it?" she asked, inwardly rolling her eyes at her own cowardice at not being able to say what she knew she should. She should just say no.

She was lying to Adam. She was lying when she pored over the all-access files on Franklin he'd given her. She was lying when she tucked away in a private file tidbits about Franklin that she would use later to connect the dots between Franklin's greed and the destruction of her father. Everyone said to follow the money, and she now had unprecedented access to just how his deep pockets had been filled with dirty money. It wasn't a complete picture yet and it wasn't pretty, but she was close. Very close.

This wasn't going to end well. Not for her and certainly not for Adam when he realized that she was only here, was only helping him because she was looking for any inroad to take down Franklin. There was no love lost between the two men and he might applaud her exposure of Franklin but Adam would never forgive the deceit that made it happen.

"Yeah, sure. You let me know."

Tess needed to fill the next few moments with some other conversation so that she didn't say something she knew she would regret.

"How does it go with your brother and sister?" It was a cheap move to change the subject to his newly found family, but she wanted to focus on the one good thing they'd done together. She selfishly needed to be reminded that she'd done something right for Adam.

"Nothing much has changed on that front. We've talked on the phone every few days, video called. I'm trying get them to come out here. Roan is on board but Sarina sends me to voicemail most of the time." Adam wiped his hands on his napkin, picked up his beer and settled back in his chair. He rubbed his face with his free hand, running his fingers through his hair in a mixed move of frustration and concern that told all the tales on how he was handling the extraordinary situation. "Let's just say that I'm much better at figuring out data analytics and computer coding than I am at being a good brother."

"No, I don't believe that." She interrupted him, not wanting him to put that on himself for one second longer. She moved over next to him, pushing his tousled hair out of his eyes, the black strands sliding silkily against her fingers. "You found them. You never stopped looking for them. That's being a *great* brother in my eyes."

"I'm not so sure that disrupting their lives is the act of a great anything. They were living…doing fine on their own and I sent you to find them, dig up all their secrets and drop a bomb right in the middle of all of it." He sighed, shaking his head. "I feel like I'm driving this reunion, doing all of this just to make myself feel better. I never had a chance to stay connected to my community, my traditions and my culture. I never had anyone ask about my life before coming to California, never had anyone try to help me remember. So…this feels…selfish. I wonder if I should just leave them alone. Let them live the lives they've made for themselves."

He looked at Tess, scanning her face for an answer she didn't even know the question for, and her heart pulled tightly for him. This man carried so much on his shoulders, she couldn't help but reach out and cover the broad expanse with her hand, giving him a squeeze in an attempt to absorb some of the tension coiled there under his skin.

"Adam," she ventured, breaking off when it was clear he had more to say.

"I found them out of guilt, you know. You never asked and I was glad you didn't because I didn't want to explain that it was all my fault. I didn't want to admit that I was the reason we were taken away."

This time she wouldn't be stopped. There was no way she letting him take the rap for what had happened. "Adam, no. Your family was blown apart because some overzealous white social workers decided that you would be better off completely ripped away from your family, your tribe, your history and your culture." He opened his mouth to speak and she placed a finger on his lips, asking him with a smile to let her finish. "These people, everyone from the social workers, to the police, to the judge, violated the Indian Child Welfare Act. *They* did this to the three of you. I did the research and I know this. Trust me."

His returning smile was dim, watered down with the regret and guilt he wouldn't release.

"I knew something bad was going to happen but I didn't tell anyone." Adam huffed out a laugh, brittle with judgment. "When I came home the night before they showed up there were owls in the trees around our house. All in the trees and it wasn't even twilight."

"I'm sorry," she asked. "I don't think I understand the importance of the owls."

"Yeah, you wouldn't. Naturally." Adam shifted in his seat, reaching out and taking a sip from his beer. His voice was low, quiet and reverent. "In the Cherokee legend—superstition I guess some people would say—the owl is a bad omen. Precursor to death or something bad that is going to happen. I should have said something and I didn't. Social Services showed up the next day and I don't remember ever seeing my family again."

She thought she understood a little bit better now. Adam thought that his not telling anyone about the owls somehow led to what happened, the destruction of his family. It sounded ridiculous, was impossible, but it would have been very real to a six-year-old boy. It would have been very real to someone whose life was based upon such tradition, such legends. It wasn't her background but she respected that it was Adam's and it was as much a part of him as her ingrained culture was a part of her own makeup.

But she couldn't let him carry this guilt. She'd read the reports and the local social workers had wrecked so many families with their blatant disregard for the sanctity of their culture and their lives. There had been countless numbers of children ripped away from their homes, and people who were sworn to protect and ensure that the laws were followed looked in the other direction at the least and abetted the tragedy at the worst. And it wasn't just in his community where this happened. All you had to do was a cursory internet search and it would spit out thousands of similar stories across the United States and Canada.

But the pain of that day and every day since then was real to Adam. The who, what, why and how were secondary to the fact that his life was never the same.

Tess reached out to him, cupping his jaw and drawing him close enough for their noses to brush in the most tender of touches. His eyes were dark and heavy with his sad memories and she wished she had the power to take some of this from him, to bear it herself.

"Adam, I'm not going to tell you that you shouldn't feel that way or try to ease your pain with a saying from a really crappy greeting card. But I'm going to tell you what I *know*. Okay?" She waited for his nod, given jerkily in between the ragged intake of deep gulping breaths. "There was nothing you could have done to stop it. And not because you were just a child, only six years old. Your parents couldn't have done anything. They weren't connected, educated, powerful. They were poor and doing their best just like every other family. They went through a rough patch and had to reach out to social services for help and got on the radar of an overzealous case worker. The people who should have done better, who should have been better, decided that your family wasn't good enough for you and your siblings. They also decided that they were above the law and the people who could have stopped them didn't. So, yes, the owl was the sign of the terrible things that were coming for your family but they were going to happen whether you told anyone or not. And *that* is the truth."

The moments slid one into the other. Adam stayed where he was, leaning on her for strength that she was ready and willing to give. It wasn't a permanent thing, wasn't a shift of what they were. This was what they were to each other, both strong people who'd had to bear more on their shoulders than what was normally required from a very young age. What they recognized was a kindred spirit, someone who understood a lot without being told.

This moment didn't change what they could and couldn't be for each other. It didn't absolve her from her lies or the guilt and it wouldn't shield her from his anger when he found out. It was just a moment. A really special moment. A few seconds of mutual understanding in the middle of a tangled mess of secrets.

"It's the truth," Adam agreed, his voice deeply etched by the remaining shards of glass that had cut him for so long. "But I don't know if I did my brother and sister a favor by finding them. I sure as hell don't know what to do with them now that they are back in my life. Family is a mystery to me."

"Well, you all have that motorcycle obsession. Maybe you do a road trip?"

He huffed out a weak laugh. "Roan would probably say yes. Sarina would take the first exit and ditch us both."

Tess sat back, taking the opportunity to push his hair back from his forehead, needing to maintain the physical connection between them. She loved touching Adam, craved the electric thrill that went through her whenever they connected. He made her feel…seen…wanted.

"Family is very hard." She gave him a sidelong glance, nervous about giving away too much of herself. Afraid to let him get too close. "I think I told you that once."

"You did." He reached up, running a finger along her brow, down her cheekbone. "Sounded like you knew what you were talking about."

Tess started shaking her head, her grin twisted with her reluctance to share. "You don't want to hear about it."

Adam leaned forward, pressing a sweet kiss to her mouth, barely a brush of lips, an exchange of breaths. "I showed you mine…come on, show me yours."

Nine

It wasn't right to push Tess.

Adam knew what it was like to have a secret you needed to keep close, parts of yourself that you didn't want to share. He'd spent his entire life after his adoption guarding his real self from the world he'd been dropped into. Adam had never fit in, he'd always been on the outside. At school. In his new home. Nobody made any effort to ask him about his past, his family, his community. He'd given up after a while; it was easier just to bury himself in the books or sports. Easier to forget the memories that crept back in at night. Easier to forget the family he'd lost.

Justin had been the first person he let in. But he'd

also been the first to give Adam the space to keep the secrets he needed to keep in order to survive.

So, he also knew how important it was to have people who respected the distance you needed to function under the weight of the secrets and the pain that went with them. But it didn't stop him from wanting to know more about this woman who occupied his thoughts and made his body hard with need with just a glance.

But he wanted to know all of her secrets, all the things she hid behind her sexy smiles and bravado. Unlike Tess's deep dive into his past, he hadn't done a full background check on her when he'd hired her. Yes, he'd asked his security to check on her and they'd run a criminal scan, verified that her business and license were in order and legitimate, and that her references checked out. He had not had them give him a full dossier on her life, her background. It had felt sordid and unnecessary and overly intrusive. But now when every part of him screamed to get closer to this woman, he wished he'd received that file.

No, that was not the way he wanted to learn all the unique and special things that made Tess Lynch a woman who kept him awake at night.

He wanted her to tell him. Willingly. Because she wanted to make this connection with him too. It wasn't keeping within their rules, just like the dinner out that he'd suggested earlier before he'd had a minute to think about it. The question had popped out, something that never happened. He wasn't someone who made a habit of speaking without thinking long and hard about it. It was his strength or his weakness, depending on who you were. His business partners loved it. The women in his life, not so much.

But as soon as he'd said it, he wanted it. More time with Tess, no matter how he could get it.

But not this way.

"You know what? Don't answer that." He tucked a curl of hair behind her ear. "You don't owe me that. Not just for listening to my story."

Tess considered him, her green eyes taking him apart inch by inch. He didn't shy away from it, he was man enough to take it. Her armor didn't scare him.

"I have a sister too," Tess began, her smile chagrined as she shook her head in an I-can't-believe-I'm-doing-this way. "Her name is Mia and she's making me prematurely gray."

"Your parents? Is it just the two of you?"

Tess nodded, breaking eye contact to pull fluff he could not see off her skirt. "My mother was gone when Mia was a year old, I was five. My father passed when I was twenty. I raised Mia."

"You got the teenage years," he noted, relieved to see a smile twist up her full lips. "Not the best luck."

"And she gave me fits. Sneaking out of the house,

terrible boyfriends, even worse clothing and hairstyle choices. It's a miracle we both survived."

"And now?"

"She's at college. Whip smart but still has horrible taste in men and clothes." Tess shrugged, her grin more genuine this time, and his stomach flipped with the impact of it. "We didn't have an easy time of it. My father was ill, mentally ill, and it made life hard at times. Mia's success is a happy ending to all of that."

"I'm so sorry. What did he do? Is Mia following in his footsteps? Did you?"

"What? No." She waved him off, weaving her fingers with his as she avoided his eyes. This was where she buried the worst of it and he'd let her keep her skeletons where they were. "He was a scientist. An inventor."

"All scientists are the kissing cousins of poets."

Tess considered that, nodding her agreement in the end. "That must be true. He was as tortured as a poet. Broken dreams haunted him, things that had been taken from him chased him to the end."

The pain in her voice was palpable, the words weaving a scent of bitterness in the air that he could almost smell and taste. There were also traces of anger in her tone. Understandable under the circumstances. Anger was something he understood very well.

"So, you see, I know firsthand that family can be hell."

Tess rose from the chair and Adam took her hand, turning it over to kiss her palm, nipping the most tender part and making her squirm. Tess giggled and he wanted more of it, standing and leaning over to press kisses along her neck, her shoulder.

He pulled back and looked down at her, pleased to see the flush in her cheeks and the sparkle in her eyes. No more heavy talk tonight. They'd lived it once, they didn't need to go through it again.

"So, dinner… Are you still thinking about? Can we be seen together in public now that I know you have a sister?" he teased, feeling the mood in the room lighten as her eyes lit up with shrewd humor.

"We just ate. How can you be hungry enough to talk about our next meal?"

"That's not what I'm hungry for right now," he said, the truth slipping out easily as the mood shifted again, sliding deeply and completely into something darker and needier.

Tess moved in closer to him, her hands sliding up his chest and around his neck, ensuring that every part of her body was flush against his.

"I love your body," he growled, running his hands up and down every part of her he could reach. Her fine, full ass. Heavy, soft breasts. The curve of her hip. The soft velvet of her skin. "It should be illegal for anyone to look like you, Tess."

"I could say the same about you, Adam Redhawk. You're tempting enough to make me break all of my rules."

"Really? You always seem to be in perfect control around me."

"Then you're not paying attention." She considered Adam, a wicked gleam darkening her eyes to the deepest emerald as she stepped in even closer. If that was possible. As it was, he wasn't sure where he began and she ended. "I think you're hot."

"Good to know, but I don't think my looks rock your control."

Tess let loose with the tiniest hint of a smile, transforming her expression into the epitome of pure sin. "Your taste. I can't get it off my tongue. I'm always craving more."

He groaned as she leaned in closer, her lips just a breath away from his own. Adam leaned in to close the distance but Tess inched back. He moved in again and she shifted back a hair's breadth, dragging another groan out of him, this one of frustration. He lifted his hands to her face, anchoring her in place as he took his turn to play the game, coming close but not sealing their mouths together.

Now it was Tess's turn to moan, her breath coming fast on a pant that heaved her breasts into his chest with every inhale. Her pulse was visibly hammering under the delicate, pale skin of her throat.

Adam dipped his head, unable to resist licking that spot, savoring her salty-sweet flavor.

"I want you to fuck me, Adam."

Damn, that was exactly what he wanted too. The only thing that would satisfy this ache building deep inside him.

"Hell, yes. I want that too. Your legs wrapped around me, your nails digging into my back. Your screams passing over these lips." Adam reached out with his tongue, tracing the full plumpness of her lips, capturing her own moan on the tip and savoring the taste of her surrender.

He glanced up at the glass walls of his office and was reminded of the reason he'd never had sex with her here. Security wouldn't be making rounds at this time of night but anybody who decided to walk by would see them.

"I should take you down to your office," he said.

"Too far. I don't care about anyone seeing us. I just want you, Adam." Tess reached down between them and ran a hand up and down the length of his erection. "I've always wanted to have you fuck me in your office."

"Damn it, Tess," he whispered, the only warning she was going to get about how this was going to go down. Hot. Intense. Passionate. The way it always was between them, but every time they touched it burned hotter the next time. Her breath caught just before he angled his head and took her mouth.

The kiss was hard and hungry, lips bruising and teeth clashing as they devoured each other. After weeks of total access to each other's bodies and mouths nothing between them had cooled down. Tess moaned into the kiss, wrapping her hands around his neck and pulling him in closer, as if her next breath depended on his being as close to her as possible. Adam echoed her movement, hands cupping her ass to drag her closer as he sought to dominate her, possess her.

With them it would never be easy, only complete and total surrender would satisfy this craving and neither of them would give in to that. They'd both been burned too much and too often.

But they'd get as close as they could, feeding off each other's need until this fire between them died.

Tess broke off the kiss first, her breasts rising and falling as she struggled to catch her breath. She licked her lips, pink and kiss swollen, and he wanted nothing more than to see them wrapped around his cock.

"I want that too. So much," Tess answered and he realized that he had spoken the words aloud.

He groaned again as her hands traveled over his body, stopping to wrap around his neck and pull him down to her. This time Tess took over the kiss, slanting her lips over his and sliding her tongue into his mouth. This time it was slower, softer, Tess exerting her power in this thing between them, controlling the gradual buildup of passion and possession. It turned him on, compelling him to slide his hands over her ass, angling their hips forward, finding the perfect position to grind his erection into her body.

It was bewitching. Intoxicating. Addictive. He explored the curves of her body with his hands, cupping her breasts in his palms, thumbs rubbing against the hard nipples straining against the soft fabric of her dress.

Tess released his mouth, her palms pressed firmly against his chest as she eased him backward toward the sofa. When his knees hit the edge of the seat cushion, she gave him a firmer push, forcing him to sprawl on the sofa, legs spread open in blatant invitation.

He wanted Tess. No hiding it.

Tess leaned over him, her lips close enough to his own that they were exchanging sharp, shallow pants of breath. Adam raised his hand, stroking up the side of her bare leg, under her skirt, under the silky material of her panties.

The first touch of his fingers against the wet, slick heat of her body had them both gasping, teeth biting into lower lips in anticipation of what was to come. The second slide of skin upon skin had Tess's eyes easing shut, her body swaying into his caress, silently begging for more. Adam kept his focus on her face, soaking in every erotic turn of her expression, burning them all into his memory.

"Ohhhhh noooo." Tess opened her eyes, stepping back and out of his reach, her head shaking back and forth. "Naughty boy. You're not going to distract me. Hands down. Stay put."

Adam chuckled at her tone, contemplating whether to let her run this show but realizing that he was never in control of any situation with Tess.

Tess walked back a few paces, staring down at him, her eyes dark emerald with need but assessing, full of all the wicked plans she had on her mind. He clenched his hands at his sides, determined to sit back and see what she would do to him.

"I feel like I'm overdressed for this activity," Tess murmured, her fingers drifting over the edge of the V-neck of her dress, between her breasts, and down to where her dress tied at the side. A quick movement and her dress opened, sliding to the floor at her feet in a swoosh of fabric and leaving her standing before him in nothing but a gorgeous black bra and panty set, a gold necklace, high heels and a sinful grin. "Much better."

Adam groaned, digging his heels into the carpet as he resisted every urge to reach out and take.

"Having that dress on would have made it so difficult to do this," Tess said, dropping to her knees in front of him, shifting onto all fours as she slowly crawled across the floor toward him.

Adam moaned, ending on what suspiciously sounded like a whimper, the dirty twist of her lips making his heart thunder in his chest and his ears. He stared at her as she covered the short distance between them, back arched like a cat and eyes locked on his own. He held his breath when she was right in front of him, releasing it on a shudder when her hands slowly slid up both of his calves to his thighs, finally ending on the swollen bulge making his pants very tight.

"Remember. My rules," Tess warned him again, her fingers hovering over his zipper until he gave a terse nod of agreement.

She undid his belt, then the button, sliding down the zipper with a metallic sound that was as loud as thunder rumbling in this office, the whole world vectored down to just the two of them. Tess's hand wrapped around him and his eyes shut hard, his groan of pleasure reverberating behind his clenched teeth, his hands tightening into fists at his sides. He willed himself to not break the rules and risk Tess stopping.

Up and down her hand glided along his length, her voice a deeper, huskier version of her typical tone. "Adam, I want this in my mouth. Can I?"

"Oh my God, yes. Please."

Adam stared down as she leaned back in and took his erection deep into her mouth. Lips clamped tight around his flesh, Tess bobbed her head up and down, the rhythm leading to a slow burn in his groin, his belly. Unable to resist the urge to touch, to thrust into her wet heat, his fingers slid into the auburn silk of her hair, his body throbbing at the sound of her whimper.

"Damn, Tess, you're so beautiful." His words cut off but the lust in her eyes, the electricity of their attraction, snapped across the distance between their bodies. And like the images burned on the back of his eyelids after a lightning strike, he knew this sight would be branded on his brain. The burn of her touch intensified until he was almost there, way too soon for how he needed this to end. "Stop. Stop, baby, I need to be inside you."

Tess moved up and over his body, kissing him hard and fierce. "All you had to do was ask."

There was nothing better than Adam Redhawk wanting her.

Tess had known enough men in her life, spent enough time in their beds to know who would forget her the minute the sheets cooled, but Adam was different. The rules were that this was going to be temporary, and she wouldn't contemplate a change to that, but she knew that he would remember this time together long after they were over. And that… that was really sexy.

And Adam was letting her push his buttons. He was known to be a control freak in the bedroom but this game of give and take between them was hot, intriguing—it kept her running hot all the time.

Adam dragged her down to part her lips with a brutal kiss before pulling her onto his lap, her legs straddling each side of his thighs. Tess gave as good as she got, digging her nails into his shoulders as he broke off the kiss, his lips wet and red and pulled back in a grin.

"I want to taste you now, Tess. My turn." He growled as he tugged down the straps of her bra, exposing her breasts to his gaze and his touch. He wasted no time, cupping them both in his palms, dragging his thumbs across the tips.

Tess let her head fall back, body thrusting forward to offer them up to him, wordlessly begging Adam to taste them. He was taking too long, teasing her nipples into hard, tight points that ached under his attention. She wasn't above begging. Not when she knew how good he could make her feel.

"Adam, please. Put them in your mouth."

He rubbed his lips against her skin, just above where she really wanted him to be. He skimmed the curve of her breast, leaving a trail of hot, moist breath as he made his way to her neck. She felt a long lick along the column of her neck, tantalizing nibbles over the places that made her jump in his arms, writhe against his body in a desperate search for more of him, more pleasure.

But even Tess had her breaking point. She growled, weaving her fingers in his hair and leading his face down to her breasts. It should have been relief, getting what she wanted, but Adam was over-whelming, licking, teasing, sucking the hard nubs of flesh into his mouth. Lightning. Fire. An ache threaded its way under her skin, running along every nerve ending in her body and setting her mind on a whirling spiral of pleasure that rose higher and higher.

Adam ran his hands down her body as the cool air of the office washed across her thighs and goose bumps added that tingle of sensation to everything else she was feeling. It was almost too much and it wasn't enough. She needed him. Needed him inside her; the lazy circles his fingertips were tracing over the sex-slick core of her body were not enough. Tess ground her body down on his touch, legs shaking, muscles flexing, seeking the orgasm she knew he could give her.

She keened, leaning heavily on him as the plea-sure made her weak. "Adam, I'm going to come."

As if those weren't the magic words that would open the door to all of her desires, Adam pulled away, releasing her flesh and removing his hands from between her legs. Tess gasped, thumping against his chest with her palms in protest.

"Damn you. I was *so* close."

"I want you to be all around me when you come, Tess," Adams growled against her lips, his kisses soft and tender, designed to soothe and tempt. "Don't you dare come right now. It's mine and that's how I want it."

She wouldn't deny that it was his. Hell, when they were together like this, she was his. Body and soul. But not her heart. She wouldn't go that far.

Tess was ready to risk the great sex and the fun they had together, the connection that always kept them tethered to each other. But she couldn't risk her heart. Her father had broken her heart. Life had shattered it over and over. She never wanted to feel that kind of helplessness ever again. Her heart was hers and it would never belong to another ever again.

But she could give Adam her pleasure.

"Then take it. Don't make me wait."

Adam shifted under her, maneuvering their bodies until she was facing the back of the sofa, legs spread with her body open to him. Tess leaned forward, resting the weight of her body on the sofa back, her ass up in invitation.

Adam leaned over body, his fingers snagging in the sides of her panties and sliding them down her legs, tossing them to the floor behind them. He trailed kisses over her skin, sweet presses of his mouth raising goose bumps all along her spine.

"You're beautiful, Tess. Can I have you? Anything I want?"

"Anything you want," Tess said, spreading her legs wider, smiling at the groan that erupted from Adam behind her.

She looked over her shoulder, taking in Adam leaning in behind her, his large hands spreading her wider. And then his tongue was on her, stroking over her core. She jumped, the first lick electric and the second causing her to push back against him, begging him for more. She closed her eyes, knowing that if she kept watching, she would come apart. Too soon. Much too soon.

Adam found her clit, his tongue executing a rhythm that was calculated to bring her to the edge. And just when she was almost there, hips mimicking his movements, he pulled back and brought her down again. Only to do it all over a few seconds later. He had her on the edge so many times that she was only need and desire and incapable of thinking of anything beyond what he was doing to her.

And just when she thought she would have to kill him for denying her what she needed so desperately, his mouth was back on her clit and she was rising and then falling down and down into a spiral of pleasure that spun out like a car spinning out of control. Tess's body went rigid, every muscle taut with her orgasm. As the pleasure released her, she went boneless, her heart racing in a body that couldn't have moved for love nor money.

Adam made it easy on her, turning her over and laying her out on the couch. The chill of the room threatened to make her shiver but he was over her, his body keeping her warm and raising her desire again, along with her temperature.

"So beautiful," Adam whispered, his words tracing along the damp skin of her neck. His kisses covered her skin, claiming every inch of her and then taking her mouth in a tangle of tongues so sweet that it made her bones ache. "Can I still have you?"

His question was so sincere. Adam was always so intent on making sure that this was what she wanted, she could never deny him. She wanted nothing more than to give him what he asked for because he made it so good for her. Every single time.

"Yes. Adam. Please."

Adam nodded, leaning back and pulling a condom out of his pocket before pushing his pants down to his thighs. He shivered a little, the office air also raising goose bumps on his skin. Tess reached out, tugging on the hem of his shirt, unbuttoning the shirt buttons she could reach, relieved when he unfastened the rest. She sighed, raking her nails across his chest, trailing them over the hard, taut muscles, the flat brown nipples. Adam sucked in a breath and she smiled, relishing the sight of the usually quiet and collected Adam Redhawk flushed and debauched, half-dressed and fully aroused.

"I need you Adam. Hurry."

Adam ripped open the packet and slid the condom over his length, leaning in until his tip pressed against her core.

"You ready?" he asked, waiting the moment necessary for her to nod, and then sliding inside her, her slickness making it an easy glide forward.

Tess wrapped her legs around his waist, drawing him as deep as he could go, indulging in the feel of him inside her and his weight on top of her. She loved this part, the time when she was surrounded by him, filled by him. It was as if there was no way to know where she ended and he began. Perfection. For one brief second.

And then Adam pulled out of her body, almost all the way, and then slid back inside. Tess clung to his back, her nails digging in, anchoring herself to him with every hard thrust. She lifted her hips, angling her body so that he could be deeper inside her, hitting all the best spots.

And then the tingle forming at the base of her spine, in the space deep inside her belly, grew with each slide of his body inside her own and suddenly she didn't want to try to control this ride. She wanted to surrender to it. She wanted it to make her come apart with no hope of being put back together.

Tess let go of her grip on Adam, raising her arms over her head and hanging onto the sofa arm behind her. Her position was deliberately submissive, offering up all of her body to Adam. She trusted him to take her where she needed to go and to be there to catch her when she came down from the high. It was in his nature to protect. Tess would be risking nothing to let this happen between them.

"Yes. Adam. Yes."

"Jesus, Tess," Adam ground out, leaning down to take her lips in a hard, wet kiss. "You make me want. I can't get enough of you."

"Good," Tess panted out, reaching back now, her fingers digging into his hip. "I can't get enough of you."

"Good. Glad I'm not alone…in this."

Tess couldn't process the meaning of his words, not now when he was filling her body and scrambling her mind.

"I need to come," she panted, her words slurred with lust and desire. "I need…"

"I know what you need," Adam growled as he wedged his hand between them, stroking her clit with every thrust. "Come on, Tess. You know what I need."

"What?"

"You," he groaned against her lips. "You."

His words flipped all her switches and she fell over the edge, her orgasm causing her entire body to shudder and buck beneath him. The pleasure was white-hot, searingly intense, and imprinted on every cell of her body.

Adam cried out above her, his body, all sleek muscle and rigid bone, going taut with his own pleasure. He collapsed against her and Tess wrapped her arms around him, ignoring the cooling of the sweat on their bodies and the knowledge that they really weren't alone in this building. She just wanted to indulge in this moment, knowing that it would end soon enough.

That was the deal they had agreed to, after all.

But maybe some of the rules could be broken.

"So…" she ventured, trailing her nails lightly up and down his back.

"Yeah?"

"About that dinner out…"

Adam lifted his head, propped himself up on an elbow to gaze down and her, and raised an eyebrow in humor. "What? All it took was a mind-blowing orgasm to get a meal out of you?"

"A girl has got to have her standards."

Ten

Tess was probably going to kill him.

Adam pulled up in front of the small bungalow tucked into the end of a small street in the solidly middle-class neighborhood. Nearby yards and driveways were littered with abandoned bikes and skateboards, anchored with basketball nets, and dotted with "Please slow down—children at play" signs. It wasn't anything like the one he'd grown up in, with locked gates and housekeepers answering the door. This was a neighborhood where the streets filled with costumed kids on Halloween and wagon parades on the Fourth of July. Adam didn't remember ever having that.

He shook off the dark cloud that always accompanied his dwelling on the ghosts of shitty childhoods past and cut the engine of his car, pausing to consider just how weird this was. Adam hadn't heard from Tess in almost two days; no response to his texts and voicemails and she'd failed to show at Redhawk/Ling. None of that sounded at all like the Tess he knew. They'd spent every waking moment together or in constant contact in the past few weeks, either searching for the mole or finding chances to work off steam in a way that left him aching for more. So, he was down to two schools of thought about what he was currently doing: it was restraining order level of stalker activity or the action of a normal, noncreepy friend/fuckbuddy.

The jury was still out on which way the "Jury of Tess" would fall on the issue.

But he kept coming back to the fact that failing to show up for work or answer his inquiries was nothing like Tess Lynch. If she didn't want to talk to you, she'd tell you to your face in unequivocal language and then freeze you out like a blizzard at the North Pole.

Screw it. If she murdered him, so be it.

Adam opened the door on his Audi R8 Spyder and glanced around the neighborhood as he shut the door. Three doors down a young woman was pretending to pull weeds as she watched him and her toddler out of the corner of her eye. She paused when she got the full look of him and her wide-eyed re-action was either because he was a stranger in her neighborhood, he was a brown stranger in her neigh-borhood or she was ogling his car. He nodded, giv-ing her his best "I'm a billionaire business owner so please don't call the cops" smile and walked up the short concrete walk lined with pretty flowers to the teal-painted front door and raised his hand to push the doorbell. He hesitated a brief moment, giving himself one more chance to back out before press-ing the button.

He could hear the perky tone of the bell chime be-hind the closed door but that was it. Not the sound of footsteps, no voice yelling at him to hang on. Noth-ing. He waited a few moments longer, shifting to try to peek through the large bay window in the front of the house but noting that the privacy blinds were shut tight. He reached out to the doorbell again, pressing on it an extra few seconds. It was irritating enough to wake the dead.

It worked because within a couple of seconds he heard the distinctive sound of Tess Lynch cursing whoever was at her door to one of the seven layers of hell. Relief loosened the knot that had settled in the bottom of his belly, only to be replaced by confusion about why Tess had decided to drop off the earth and out of his life. And out of his bed…well, his couch.

"Who is it?" Tess asked through the door and even

with the solid wood barrier between them, Adam could tell that her voice was rough and scratchy.

"It's Adam. Are you all right?"

There was a brief pause and then the sound of the locks releasing followed by the door sliding open. He was greeted by a disheveled Tess, eyes red rimmed and cheeks flushed, glaring at him across the threshold. Her hair was a tangled mass of red curls and her pajamas looked like she'd been wearing them a few days. Of course, the absolute wrong thing fell out of his mouth.

"Tess, you look terrible."

The door slammed in his face with a ferocity that rattled the glass in the side lights.

"Tess, wait." He twisted the knob, grateful when it gave way and the door swung open. She hadn't locked him out. He stepped inside and spotted her retreating back as she shuffled down a hallway, rushing forward when she swayed and reached for the wall in a move to steady herself. He slid his hands around her waist, murmuring against her temple, "I've got you."

Tess was burning up, her skin hot and clammy to the touch. She leaned on him, accepting his support as he guided her around the corner into an open plan kitchen and family room. Adam picked up Tess and carried her over to the sofa, ignoring her indignant protest and attempts to wriggle out of his arms before he lowered her onto the bright yellow cushions.

"*Stay there.* I'll go get you some water." He strode over to the refrigerator, noting the sleek lines and warm colors of her home as he searched the cabinets until he located a glass and filled it with cold water. He moved back toward the sofa, relieved to see that Tess hadn't wandered off. He eased down next to her and placed the glass in her hands. "Take a drink. You need to stay hydrated with a fever."

"I'm fine," she insisted, taking a few large swallows before handing the glass back to him. She was pale, and her voice was scratchy when she gave him as much hell as she could muster. "What are you doing here, Adam?"

"You haven't been seen or heard from in a couple of days. I was worried. You could have been taken by a serial killer." He shrugged, feeling heat settle in his own cheeks at her piercing stare. "I wanted to make sure you were okay."

"How did you find out where I live?" she asked, taking another sip of water when he nudged the glass back toward her mouth.

"I employ a lot of people who are good with computers."

She narrowed her eyes at him. "That's pretty shady shit for you, Adam Redhawk. Illegal even."

"Well, the only other option was to call the police and ask for a wellness check and I figured that would get me murdered by you at the first opportunity."

"You're right." Tess set down the water glass on

the coffee table and wiped her face with a shaking hand. "But, I'm fine. I just need to rest and I can't do that with you here."

Tess stood and swayed again, her body tensing when he gathered her against his body. She wasn't going to make this easy.

"Look, let me help you take your meds and fix you something to eat." She opened her mouth to argue with him but he cut her off with a shake of his head. She wasn't going to win this argument because he was pulling out the big guns. "No. I'm not leaving until I know you're okay or I'm going to call your sister."

"Oh, you suck." Tess glared at him but she sagged against him in defeat. Whether that was just from the illness or the threat, he didn't know and he didn't care.

"Well, get over it." He scanned the kitchen island for signs of any pill bottles or medicines. "When are you due for another dose of meds?"

Tess groaned and leaned her forehead against his chest, her already-scratchy voice muffled against the fabric of his shirt. "My doctor called in an antibiotic but I fell asleep and haven't gone to pick it up yet."

"Tess, you're running a fever. You need the meds." Adam bit back asking her why she didn't call him but he knew the answer: they were just sleeping together. You didn't call the current fling and ask them to pick up medication at the pharmacy. And with her sister at school, Tess wasn't going to reach out to anyone else. It wasn't in her nature to ask for help. Adam tucked her close to him again as he reached for his phone. "I'll call someone to bring it here."

Her head whipped up. "Not Estelle."

"No, I wouldn't ask anyone from the company to come over here. Trust me." He looked around, trying to gauge where her bedroom was located. "Why don't you grab a shower while I fix you something to eat?"

"I'm not hungry," she mumbled as she moved toward the hallway.

"You'll need to eat with the antibiotic. Go shower and leave the rest to me." Adam pointed toward the hallway, while thumbing across the screen of his phone and hitting the number for the person he knew would help him out.

"You're so bossy," Tess grumbled once more before she turned the corner. He smiled a little at her stubbornness and decided that he'd let her have the last word. She was sick after all.

A short phone call later and he was following Tess's path down the hallway, listening for the sound of running water. The second door to the right was open, which led to her bedroom. He went in, turning on the overhead light and taking his first look around the space where Tess slept.

It was small for a master bedroom but in proportion to the scale of the cottage. But what it lacked in size, it more than made up for in comfort and style. Three walls were painted a warm honey color with the fourth decked out in a Mediterranean blue, giving the room the feeling of warm days on a beach in Greece. The comforter was a deep oceanic blue and pillows in white, silver and lighter shades of blue were scattered over the bed around the Tess-shaped spot on the left side of the mattress.

Ducking back out into the hallway, Adam grabbed a new set of sheets and proceeded to strip down the bed and remake it, stacking the decorative pillows on a large armchair in the corner next to the large window that faced the small fenced backyard. Adam could just spy a small patio filled with a table and chairs and a grill.

Hearing the water turn off on the shower, he moved toward the open door to the adjoining bathroom, leaning against the door frame as Tess finished wrapping a large towel around her long, lush body. Her hair was wet and darkened to the deepest shade of auburn, the strands sticking to the damp, heat-pinkened skin of her shoulders. Adam remembered the silk of her flesh, the sweet taste of her sighs as he kissed her all over.

Now she had no makeup. No hairstyle. No sexy outfit.

Tess Lynch was still the most beautiful woman he'd ever seen.

She looked over her shoulder at him and he could

see the bone-deep fatigue in the lines around her mouth and the lack of brilliance in her eyes. And just like that the pull was back in his chest, the one that made it difficult to take a deep breath. Adam leaned against the door frame, willing his heart to revert to its normal rhythm and his tongue to form the right words.

"Your medicine is on the way. I'll be in the kitchen making you something to eat."

"Adam." Tess sighed in exasperation, the hoarse whisper barely traveling across the room to where he stood. She shuffled forward a couple of paces, closing the distance between them to less than arm's length. "Why are you doing this?"

She was tired but the suspicion etched into the rigid lines of her body and the doubt clouding her gaze were unmistakable. He reached out, lightly brushing wet curls off her forehead. "Don't get too worked up—I'm not that great a cook."

Tess shook her head and he knew she wasn't going to make this easy. "This is not what we agreed to. This is not something you do for a fuckbu—"

Adam stopped her with his thumb pressed gently to her lips. Yeah, he'd thought the same thing just a few moments before but he didn't want to hear it from her. He didn't want to think too hard on why he didn't like being shoved into a category he'd initially suggested either. Not today.

"Hey, we've got a friends with benefits thing

going on…" He pushed off the door frame and turned to head back toward the kitchen. "Today I'm doing the friend thing. Don't overthink it, Tess. Get dressed and come get something to eat."

Adam searched her kitchen for something that he could prepare and not make Tess feel worse. He wasn't a terrible cook but he did only a certain number of dishes well enough to serve to anybody else and those consisted of things you could grill and an omelet. A quick check of the fridge yielded eggs and cheese. Good. He wouldn't have to order takeout.

Her kitchen was small but well organized and he found a skillet and all the utensils he needed. He cracked the eggs, shredded the cheese and concentrated on cooking and not on the real reason he was there in Tess's kitchen breaking all the rules.

"Now, that's something I never thought I'd see," Tess said as she entered the kitchen. She walked slowly, clearly not feeling well but looking fresh and beautiful in a set of emerald green pajamas. He nodded toward one of the bar stools pulled up to the island, smiling when she didn't argue with him.

"What's that?"

"A billionaire in my kitchen, cooking for me."

He chuckled, using the spatula to do the perfect flip over of the cooked eggs. "No, it's just me. Adam."

"Just Adam," she said, her eyes tracking his every move. "Who is that guy?"

Tess was trying to figure him out and he hoped she was successful and then explained it all to him. He hadn't known who he was since she'd walked into his office, since he'd found his family.

"When you figure it out, let me know." Adam avoided her gaze, it was too piercing, too knowing. Not today. He offered up another topic to take the spotlight off of him. "Roan agreed to come out here and spend some time together."

"That's good, Adam. Really good."

"He's wrapping up a commission and then he has to go to some party in Monaco or some other place with a palace." He smiled, remembering how his little brother acted like hanging out with celebrities was no big deal. "He's going to come out here after that is all wrapped up."

"And Sarina?"

He paused, gathering his thoughts as he checked underneath the egg, cheese and veggie mixture. Almost done. "I don't know if that's going to happen. I can't…" Adam swallowed hard, clearing his throat and trying to relax the ball of anxiety lodged in his gut. "I can't seem to reach her."

"Out of the three of you, she's been alone most of her life. She got lost in the system, fell through the cracks. She had to be there for herself because there was nobody else." Tess tapped the countertop to get him to look at her. "She's worth it. Trust me. She's not rejecting you…it's how she survives."

And somehow Adam knew that Tess was also talking about herself. Whether she intended to or not.

"I won't give up. I'm not built that way." He plated the omelet and scooted it across the island toward Tess just as the doorbell rang. "I already poured some orange juice for you. That's your meds. Eat."

"You're so bossy today."

Adam hustled down the hallway and grabbed the medication from the courier, giving him a huge tip before shutting the door. He was already reading the directions on the side of the bottle when he turned the corner.

"Take this huge horse pill every eight hours for the next five days and you'll be back to kicking my ass before you know it." He placed one in front of her on the counter, pleased to see that she'd eaten most of the omelet. "And then it's back to bed for you."

"Bossy." Tess took the pill, glaring at him as he disposed of the food and put the dirty dishes in the dishwasher.

"Bed." He held out his hand, shocked that she took it so quickly but going with it. He led her down the hallway and to her bed, then pulled back the comforter and helped her slide between the sheets. Adam tucked the covers around her, smiling down at the goofy, sleepy grin on her face.

"You changed my sheets."

"Uh-huh. Nobody likes to get into a bed with dirty sheets when they're sick."

"Adam." She started to argue with him but the yawn that racked her body took out any of the sting in the tone of that one word. "Don't get used to this. You're not the boss of me."

"Yeah, well, I think you need someone to boss you around sometimes."

"Adam, don't psychoanalyze me." Tess reached out and pushed the hair off his forehead, letting her finger trail down his nose, across his lips. He reached up and grabbed her hand, kissing the tips of her fingers.

"I've got you figured out a little, Tess. Neither one of us likes to let people take care of us but we spend most of our time taking care of everybody else." He kissed her fingers again, then gently tucked her hand underneath the covers, taking a moment to press a kiss to her forehead and then the tip of her nose. "Let me do this. I promise we'll never speak of it again. It will be our secret."

She nodded, her lids already heavy with fatigue as she snuggled down under the covers.

Adam leaned down one more time, pressing a kiss to her hair, breathing in the unique and completely addictive scent of Tess. She was argumentative, stubborn, difficult and the most frustrating woman he'd ever met but he couldn't shake her. He wanted to know all of her secrets and to create a million more that were just between them.

And for some reason, those thoughts didn't scare him as much as he thought they should.

Eleven

"Tess, why is there a strange, hot dude in your chair?"

Tess struggled against the weight of sleep and weariness and medication to get to the surface and answer the voice that accompanied the hand currently shaking her shoulder. She wiped a hand across her eyes, clearing away the gritty layer on her lashes and blinking into the pale light sneaking through the slats in her blinds. She stretched a little, testing out her body, and assessed that she didn't feel one hundred percent but she did feel much better than yesterday.

"Tess, are you okay? Is that Adam Redhawk?" Mia's face came into focus, her expression filled with equal doses of concern and curiosity.

"Mia, what are you doing here?" It was the middle of the semester and it was uncommon for her sister to make a trip home so close to midterms.

"I came home to get some quiet to study and found an expensive-as-shit-car in the driveway, you out cold in bed and him over there." Mia pointed to the oversized chair across from her bed and to the man currently sprawled out on it.

Adam's large frame made the chair look small and very uncomfortable. He was slumped down onto the cushions, his long legs spread out before him, a too-small throw blanket tucked up under his chin. His hair was a mess, falling over into his face and obscuring his eyes but leaving visible the five o'clock shadow darkening his jaw. He looked different in his sleep as everyone did but his vulnerability and rugged handsomeness struck her as if she'd never seen him before.

And she'd never seen him like this. When they were together it was never in a bed, never overnight. She'd never woken up with him wrapped around her, never had the chance to watch him when all of his defenses were down and it was just the man.

What a mistake. She'd missed one of the best parts.

"Sis, are you okay? I saw a prescription on the kitchen counter. Are you sick?" Mia intruded into her thoughts, stopping her from going down a path that she knew led to nowhere she belonged.

Tess circled back over the last day, recalling Adam showing up at her door, cooking the omelet, taking care of her. He'd stayed while she slept, waking her in the night to give her a second dose of the antibiotic and tucking her back into bed. And he must have stayed all night.

"I am… I was sick. Caught something and got an infection." She shoved off the covers, sitting up in bed to facilitate her coming back to the land of the living. She waved in the general direction of the man currently the topic of discussion. "Adam stopped by to make sure I was okay. He…helped me out…must have stayed overnight."

"Uh, okay." Mia's face showed the considerable effort it took for her to digest everything she'd just heard. She sputtered with words, not bothering to disguise her confusion. "Wow. That's really nice." And then her eyes flew open, brows shooting halfway to her hairline. "Whoa, are you two…? I mean that's something you only do for close friends and people you're fu—"

Tess's hand whipped out almost on autopilot and covered Mia's mouth. They were not going to have this discussion with Adam only a few feet away.

"I think this might be the best time for me to let you know that I'm awake."

Adam's deep voice rumbled out from the direction of the chair and both she and Mia jumped and spun around to watch him as he stretched, arms and legs flexing with the effort of waking. His shirt lifted up and they both caught a good, long look at his gorgeous skin and cut abs. Tess knew that body, knew that he'd be warm and silky and she knew exactly what was at the end of the delicious treasure trail of dark hair.

"Good morning," Mia said, her smirk indicating that her thoughts were walking the same path. Tess jabbed her with a finger, fuming when she was ignored and all Mia's attention stayed on their guest. "I'm Mia."

Adam let out a sleepy chuckle and shook the hand her sister offered. "I'm Adam and I knew who you were."

"Oh yeah? Tess show you a picture of me?" Tess rolled her eyes at the antics of her soon-to-be-dead little sister. She remained braced to tackle her to the ground if this conversation took a turn for the worse.

"No. You two are identical. I'd know you anywhere." Adam rose, his hands busy with folding the blanket and draping it over the arm of the chair.

"Because we're both so gorgeous?" Mia asked, her eyes flashing with humor and mischief.

"Mia!" Tess was only going to put up with this one more minute and then she was going to become an only child.

Adam laughed, shuffling over to press the back of his hand on her forehead, assessing her with an allover gaze that had her leaning into his touch before she could remind her treacherous body that her sister was present. It wasn't as if Mia hadn't seen Tess with a guy before but she wasn't positive that all of the emotions, the feelings she had for Adam tumbling around inside her wouldn't be evident to anyone looking. And Mia was looking.

"Definitely gorgeous." Adam smoothed her hair back from her face, tangling his fingers in her curls and tucking one behind her ear. It was such a cheesy move but the flutter in her stomach told her that it was working. Damn him. "How are you feeling? I think your fever finally broke."

Tess reached up to touch her own cheek, her fingers brushing against and then intertwining with his before she realized what she was doing. Hell, make a meal and change her sheets and she became a total sap for this guy.

"I'm better. You can go."

He smirked but didn't move.

"Thank you." Tess put some emphasis on it, sincerity with a touch of "please go before my sister starts asking too many questions."

"Okay. I get it. Just promise that you'll call me if you need anything."

"Mia is here." She nodded toward her sister as a reminder to herself more than Adam. He nodded in return, making a move to let her hand go but she tightened her grip, giving it a squeeze. "Thank you, Adam. I'm sorry I was so much trouble—this isn't what you signed up for."

He glanced over his shoulder, his eyes full of humor and his voice lowered when he turned back. "I told you, I was just focusing on the friends part of the arrangement."

Tess sucked in a breath, loving the way his thumb rubbed along her wrist and the ripples of pleasure that raced under her skin. Adam Redhawk was dangerous. She needed to remember that but it was damn easy to forget when he was this close and was looking at her like she was Christmas and his birthday all wrapped up in one package.

He pressed a discreet kiss to the same place he'd just been caressing. She felt the heat rise in her cheeks and she knew it wasn't the fever returning, exhaling when he dropped her hand and took a step back.

"I'm going to go since you've got a very capable nurse." Adam turned to address Mia. "She needs to finish all of her antibiotics and is due for another dose in a half hour and she needs lots more rest. Don't let her tell you that she's better and can go back to work or anything."

"Now, wait a minute," Tess objected, not liking the teaming of these two for one second.

Mia held up a hand to shush her. "No to work. Yes to drugs. Got it."

Tess continued to object. She wasn't a child and she would know when she was ready to back to work. "He's not a doctor, you know."

"I got my degree at WebMD," Adam teased, backing toward the doorway like a man who was well versed in self-preservation. "Don't come to the office for a couple of days, Tess. Don't make me alert security to get you off the property. Call me."

"I owe you one," she answered, never wanting to be in anyone's debt but knowing when it was true.

"If you insist," he said, giving a salute as he disappeared around the corner.

Tess watched him leave, listening to his footfalls on the hallway floors and the sound of the door closing before she turned to her sister.

Mia beat her to the punch. "Don't even try to bully me into letting you go back to work or to stop taking your meds. I'm your little sister but not an idiot."

"I'm going to take my meds." Tess hustled by her sister, leaving the room in a huff that she didn't try to hide.

She was still sick, weak, flustered and confused by everything that had happened the last couple of days. And while she was glad Mia was here, she didn't want to have the conversation her sister was going to poke and prod to have with her. It wasn't that she wanted to hide stuff from Mia but there were lots of things that she hadn't figured out herself. Like how to keep Adam's trust and do what she needed to do to bring down Franklin Thornton. Like how Adam was quickly becoming important to her.

"Tess, you can take your meds and also tell me what the hell Adam Redhawk was doing in your room all night." Mia followed on her heels like one of those annoying yappy dogs who never gave up when they had a good bone on offer.

She made her way around the kitchen island, automatically going for the coffee maker but rethinking it when her stomach gave a little gurgle. Juice sounded way more appealing, and she busied herself grabbing it from the refrigerator along with bread for toast, and avoided the intense stare of her sister across the island. She popped the bread into the toaster oven and reached for the antibiotic, taking one as prescribed and washing it down with the orange juice.

"So...how long have you been sleeping with Adam Redhawk?"

"Wow. Way to go easy on the sick person." Tess flipped her the bird and grabbed the butter from the fridge. "He was just here to help me out. He knew you were at school." She shrugged as she spread some butter on the toast. "He's just a nice guy."

"And he's sleeping with you." Mia reached over and twisted a piece of bread off and popped it into her mouth. "It was obvious from the way you let him fuss all over you. You never let anyone do that."

"And you jumped to the sex conclusion?" Mia stared at her, her expression communicating that she could do this all day and Tess knew she could. Mia didn't fall far from the stubborn tree in this family. Tess slid into the seat next to her sister, crunching down on the toast to buy some time. "It's been a few weeks."

"A few weeks?" Mia threw her hands up and mimicked throttling her sister around the throat. "And I'm just hearing about this now? My sister is dating—"

"Oh no." Tess shook her head, nipping this misunderstanding in the bud. "We are *not* dating."

"So, you're a booty call? A one-and-done?"

Tess tossed down her toast onto the plate. "Holy crap, Mia. I know you're in college but I don't want to even think about the idea that you know what any of that means."

"Tess, I'm twenty-one and a sexually active woman. So, wrap your head around that fact and tell me that *you* know what you're doing." Mia's hand covered hers and Tess wondered when that had happened. It was just yesterday when Mia's tiny, sticky fingers were engulfed by Tess's and life had been busier but a lot less complicated. "I don't want to see you get hurt."

Tess swallowed hard, Mia's words echoing the whispers that had already been circling in the back of her mind. But if she wasn't ready to deal with them in her own head, she wasn't ready to do it with her sister. The one she was supposed to be taking care of and not the other way around.

Tess patted Mia's hand, another gesture that brought back memories of earlier days. "It's just an arrangement." She leveled her with a stare that did nothing to wipe the all-knowing grin off her face. "Not a booty call. An arrangement between two consenting adults."

"Is one of those consenting adults still unaware of the vendetta the other consenting adult has aimed at his adopted father?"

Tess picked up her toast, taking a bite and grimacing at how the butter had congealed as the bread cooled. She chewed it anyway, forcing it down with juice and scrambling for an answer that would get her sister to drop it. With a sigh, she turned and faced off with Mia.

"Look, I know very well how this is likely to go. But it's what needs to be done and I promise you that I'm not taking anything on that I can't handle. Okay?"

Mia stared her down, her eyes scanning every inch of Tess's face for something she needed to see. But for once Tess didn't know how to give it to her.

Finally, Mia nodded and leaned over to press a kiss to her cheek. "You're not invincible Tess. I saw how you two looked at each other and you're headed for a whole lot of hurt if you insist on going after Franklin Thornton. I don't want to be right but you know I am."

And Tess did know. She just didn't have any choice.

Twelve

"Tess, I need to call in that favor."

The silence over the phone line did not bring Adam the comfort he was seeking. He was in a full-on panic and didn't even attempt to hide the fact. He was willing to grovel for what he needed. He'd faced down irate investors and the wrath of Franklin Thornton but this shit was scary.

"Tess, are you there?" He heard noises on the other end of the phone. A printer printing, a news program running in the background. What he didn't hear was the woman he'd called for help.

She was at home, where she'd been working since her illness a week ago. Adam still wanted her to rest. Tess wanted to go back to work. This was the compromise.

"I'm trying to remember when I agreed that I owed you a favor," Tess drawled into the line and he could picture her leaning back in her office chair, dressed in that sexy, green body-hugging dress he'd seen her in at Redhawk/Ling. She'd stopped him in his tracks, completely well and in total control of her sultry, confident and stunning beauty. Justin had laughed at him but he couldn't have given less of a shit.

Tess was beautiful. She was his—temporarily. And he needed her help.

"Tess, don't mess with me here. Sarina and Roan are coming over for dinner and I don't know what the hell I'm doing." Adam took a deep breath and willed her to help him. He hoped she wouldn't make him beg but he wasn't above it for this situation. "I need your help, Tess. I don't think I can do this by myself."

The seconds passed by way too slowly for his heart or his mental health but eventually he heard the words he'd been dying to hear.

"I'm on my way."

Forty-five minutes later his knees almost gave out with relief when his doorbell rang. He sprinted down the short hallway into the foyer and ripped the door open.

Tess stood there, now dressed in a pretty green

sundress with tiny yellow flowers embroidered all over it and flower-covered flip-flops. Her creamy pale shoulders were exposed by the way she wore her long red hair pulled up in a thingy that only let stray curls cascade down over her skin. She was delectable and enticing and his entire body went on high alert.

It had been over a week since they'd been together, her recuperation, work and his travel to Washington, DC, to vet some potential future business partners, putting up an insurmountable barrier to every need he had to taste her, touch her, make her sigh with her own pleasure around him. And now he had a bunch of family he'd not seen in fifteen years coming over and any private time reconnecting with Tess would have to wait.

"Jesus, Tess, thanks for coming over." He ushered her inside with hands *this close* to shaking. Once the door was shut behind her he clenched them into tight, almost painful fists to resist the urge to reach out and touch her.

"Hey, Adam. Come here." Tess took a step forward and suddenly her arms were around him and her lips were on his and the entire world stopped spinning at light speed. Her mouth was soft, lips parting under his, her breasts pressed against his chest, and he was surrounded by the sweet-sharp scent of her perfume. It was like the closest thing he had to coming home and immediately he was centered. Not calm but not ready to crawl out of his skin.

Too soon, way too soon, she broke the contact and smiled up at him, her grin sly enough to scare him but dirty enough to distract him from the nerves hanging out on the rough edge of his sanity. She was exactly what he needed.

"I've met both Sarina and Roan and I know they're sitting somewhere right now freaking out too. You know that, right?" Tess reassured him. "This is going to be a rough night for all of you but you'll be okay. Are you cooking?"

"Yes."

"An omelet?"

He laughed, brushing a kiss across her lips. "No, steak. The only other thing I can cook."

"It will be great." She turned in his arms, gaze traveling around the interior of his home. "Nice place. Give me a tour?"

"Sure." Adam slid his hand down her arm, enjoying the slide of their skin together and the intertwining of their fingers as he led her through his house.

Her bright dress and curls were a stark contrast to the various shades of gray and silver the designer had used all over the house and for the first time he understood why Justin said that it was cold. It was like the rest of his life, only a place to pass though in between work and more work. Tess's presence made it all feel drab somehow.

The foyer spilled over into the great room, detours leading to a home office for him just off to the left, and three bedrooms upstairs. Tess peeked inside all the rooms but he didn't let her linger, tugging her toward the back of the house and his favorite part. The main reason why he'd bought the house in the first place.

"You've got to see the best part."

"Oh my God, Adam. This is incredible." Tess let go of his hand, dropping her purse on the dining table as she sprinted over to the three-story, floor-to-ceiling windows that spanned the entire width of the house.

The El Sereno Open Space Preserve sprawled out in front of them in every possible direction. Rolling hills of green, dissected by nature trails, and flowers blooming everywhere was the view that had convinced him to buy this house. But the woman standing in front of the window eclipsed all of it.

"Can I go outside?" Tess was looking at him over her shoulder, her hand poised on the handle for the sliding glass door that led out to the wraparound deck.

"Of course."

He laughed when she gave a little hop of excitement and pulled open the door. It wasn't a typical Tess-like reaction but he had a feeling that he'd seen the "real" Tess in that moment. The one who was buried under her loss and pain and well-earned cynicism. And if this were a real relationship, he'd look forward to coaxing out more of those moments from this fascinating woman.

And more and more he wanted this to be a real relationship. There was a reason why he'd called Tess and it wasn't because she owed him one.

Adam followed her out onto the deck, past the large table and the outdoor kitchen to the railing that edged the space. Past the overly large couch and the comfortable chairs. She smiled into the waning afternoon sun, her eyes darting everywhere as she soaked it all in.

"This is why I bought this house," he said, leaning against the railing but watching her. He'd seen that view a million times but this one was better.

"And you would have been crazy not to. This is just unbelievable." Tess looked over at him, glancing back toward the interior of the house and then waving at the view. "This is more 'Adam' than the inside. Interior decorator?"

"Yeah," he answered, guessing she had the same opinion as Justin about the inside of his house. "She really liked gray."

"Obviously."

The doorbell chime brought them both up short, his smile vanishing as fast as the sun was slipping behind the mountains.

"I got this," Tess murmured and he didn't even try to stop her as she headed back through his house and quickly returned into view with two strangers who should have been family all along.

Roan was first, his swagger already recognizable

from the videos of him on YouTube. Adam's little brother was an up-and-coming name in *the* art circles and he was painting and sleeping his way through the male and female populations of the rich and glamorous. Adam had expected his confidence, cocky smile and open curiosity but what he wasn't prepared for was the doubt in his gaze and that immediately made Adam relax just a little.

He wasn't the only one feeling ill at ease about this meeting.

Sarina was a tougher character and everything about her posture kept everyone at arm's length. Newly separated from the army, she stood ramrod straight, her gaze remote and her expression aloof. Adam could imagine how intimidating she'd been as a military cop and how she'd been very good at her job. Why she'd left a successful career in the military was a question he had no idea how to answer. His more immediate concern was that nothing about her said she wanted to be here and that pierced him to the core.

"Thanks for coming to dinner." Adam gestured awkwardly around the space, feeling as clunky as his first day in every foster home and every new school. He looked toward Tess for help and she nodded, understanding everything in the briefest of glances, taking over the situation.

"It's so nice. Why don't you all sit out here? Tell

me what you'd like and I'll bring out a round of drinks and Adam can throw the steaks on the grill."

Drink orders relayed to Tess, they all watched her leave, the only person they had in common at this point, and the silence that erupted between them was as heavy as the fog that often coated the preserve in the mornings. In unison, Sarina and Roan slid out their chairs and took a seat and Adam busied himself pulling the steaks out of the outdoor fridge and firing up the grill.

"I didn't realize that you and Ms. Lynch were together," Roan said, smooth as silk but edged with a little bit of suspicion.

"No, we're not together. We're…" Adam said, eyeing Tess's progress on the drinks through the window. It was the truth but he didn't want to hurt her, didn't want her to think that he was dismissing her impact in his life. "We're friends and I thought it might be good to have her here. She's the most recent thing we all have in common."

"She knows all of our secrets, you mean," Sarina stated, her tone flat but also disapproving.

Adam and Roan exchanged a look; whether it was one of solidarity or sympathy he wasn't sure but he was grateful for it.

Tess emerged from the house a couple of minutes later and handed out the drinks before settling into a chair at the table. She'd had the foresight to turn on the sound system so they had some background music to accompany the world's most painful dinner party.

"Is this your first time in California?" she asked them in an obvious attempt to start conversation. Sarina didn't answer, only shaking her head in the negative before bringing her glass to her lips and casting her gaze over the preserve. Adam wondered why she was here. Curiosity? Obligation? Of one thing he was certain: gone was the happy, smiling toddler who teased the edges of his fuzzy memories, and that made him unspeakably sad and angry.

Roan took a drink from his beer before replying, "I've been here a couple of times. Never to this area, though. I mostly end up in LA, visiting galleries." He gestured toward the preserve. "But I love to hike and this is gorgeous. I'll have to come back and check it out."

Adam ventured a suggestion, uneasily offering a tentative connection to this stranger. "Maybe we could go out together. I'm not much of a hiker but I think I can keep up."

"You're a runner, a triathlete. I'm sure you can keep up," Roan said, his grin genuine and startlingly like his own. He turned toward Sarina, his twin, obviously trying to bring her into the conversation. They'd been separated from each other, a cut that had to run deep but you'd never know it from his brother's demeanor. Adam envied his ease. Roan might be faking it but his charm was working on him. Not so much with their sister from the shuttered look on her face. "What about you, Sarina? Might be fun."

"I don't hike. We didn't have time for that when I was growing up and even less when I was in the army," she said. Her tone didn't say the conversation was closed but nothing about it kept the ball rolling.

He mentally flipped through the report Tess had given him about his sister. She'd had it the worst of all of them: bad adoptive family, every reason to the get the hell out as soon as she could. And she'd been lucky to get out. Been lucky to last long enough to get out. Adam's gut tightened again at the recollection of facts that he could not change and he turned back to the grill, flipping the steaks and controlling what he could.

Adam plated the New York strips and took them over to the table, placing one in front of each of his guests. He grabbed the salad out of the fridge and transferred it and the various dressings to the table as well. It wasn't a four-course meal but it would give them all something to do with their hands and mouths.

They ate in silence for a few moments only occasionally making noises about how good it was. Sarina was markedly silent, pushing her food around her plate in an unconvincing show of eating. Adam had known this wasn't going to be easy but this barely sheathed hostility was impossible to penetrate and frustrating as hell. He wasn't the enemy but her cold shoulder made him feel like he was.

Even with Roan and Tess carrying the conversational load, they were done quickly and left staring at each other across the table as the evening slid into twilight. Tess reached out under the table, the weight of her hand on his leg, and the smile she offered centered him and his thoughts.

"Tess tells me that we have a mutual love of motorcycles. Harleys in particular." Adam looked at his brother and sister, relieved to see Roan's enthusiastic agreement and resigned to Sarina's exasperated nod. She didn't roll her eyes but it was pretty close.

He hadn't come this far, hadn't invested this much blood, sweat, money and tears into finding his brother and sister to watch his dreams die a quick and dirty death at this table. It was his responsibility to bring this family back together and he'd do everything in his power to make it happen.

"Our father, he loved riding a motorcycle." Adam dug into his memories, hoping to find something they could build a future on. "We had this carport attached to the house and he would spend hours out there, restoring this old Harley he'd bartered off a guy passing through the Qualla Boundary. Dad was good with his hands, could fix almost anything, and I'd sit with him and hand off the tools he needed."

Adam shook his head, surprised at his own memories. It had been years since he'd recalled that moment and he could smell the scent of grease and sunshine and the neighbors cooking sausages on a grill in their yard. How had he forgotten it?

Without thinking, he reached down and took Tess's hand in his own, comforted by the way her warmth infused his entire body with peace and assurance that this was worth it. What was happening at this table was important. And he wasn't just thinking about his brother and sister.

Tess was important and he knew the real reason he wanted her here. He wanted her to be a part of this future, his future.

"I remember when he finally finished the work on his bike and it needed a paint job in the worst way but it wouldn't keep him from firing it up and taking it for a ride." He smiled wider as the memory came more sharply into focus. "Our mom came running out of the house and yelled at him to stop doing doughnuts in the yard and he blew her a kiss and took off down the road. The bike was a piece of shit and the dust was flying but I thought he looked like the coolest guy I'd ever seen. That was when I fell in love with motorcycles."

"I think I have a photograph of him on that bike back at my place. It was in a bunch of stuff that ended up in my bag when we were taken," Roan said, his hands waving around in excitement. "I'll dig it up and make a copy." His glance widened to include Sarina. "I'll make one for all of us."

The sharp scrape of metal chair legs against the desk made them all jump and Adam swiveled to find Sarina standing, her expression stormy and her jaw set in an angry line. Adam rose to his feet, automatically reaching out to his sister, but her razor-sharp flinch from him kept him on his side of the table. Adam dropped his hand and braced for impact. If he knew anything about his sister, she wasn't going to come in slow and sweet.

"Sarina, are you okay?" Roan asked, his own chair tipping backward on two legs with his agitation. He reached back, catching it before it slammed to the ground and putting it right.

Sarina tossed her napkin on the table, empty hand slicing across the air in front of her body as if she was cutting all of the tenuous ties between them. Adam's heart dropped to the depths of the valley of the preserve. He knew what she was going to say and while he didn't want to hear it, he knew he needed to let her have it out. In reality, he didn't really have a choice. He might have brought them all together but that had ended any control he'd had over the situation and how it would end.

"Adam." She glanced at Roan, implicitly including him in her comments before sliding her gaze back to him. "You seem like a nice guy but I don't know you and I don't remember any of this happy family stuff you're spouting off like it's some movie of the week. I don't remember the motorcycle or the car-port or our mom or the fucking house. None of it."

"Sarina."

She ignored him, the hand she'd raised to silence him slowly curving into a fist. "I only remember where I ended up and if I started sharing those tales we'd all need something stronger than what you've got." Sarina took a deep breath and pressed her hands against her stomach, as if she was keeping those memories inside her, physically preventing them from coming out. "I just can't do this. I *don't want* to do this."

The silence that descended between them now felt impenetrable, worse than it had before, but he couldn't just leave it like this. He took a step forward and a huge risk by reaching out to touch her arm. Sarina's eyes narrowed with wariness and she let it sit there for a couple of seconds before taking one step backward. He let his hand drop but maintained eye contact with this woman who had his mouth and Roan's eyes.

"I won't say that I understand exactly where you are but I think I get most of it. Something really shitty happened to us, *all of us*, something that should have never happened and none of our lives were ever the same. And I understand that you were so young that you don't remember but I do. I *remember*. I remember your long hair and how you used to braid flowers and follow me around begging for piggyback rides. Those memories, my memories, I'm not ready to give them up."

"But this isn't about you and your fucking memories. This is about how you decided that we all needed to get dragged into your therapy-induced experiment. Well, I didn't ask to be part of your 'closure' or whatever the hell you're doing here. I didn't ask to be part of any of this."

He couldn't have filled the silence that followed because he didn't have anything else to say. Adam didn't have the answers, didn't know how to fix this, and that made him want to howl at the rapidly rising moon.

But Sarina wasn't looking for answers. From the sharp concrete-hard set to her mouth, he knew she wasn't going to relent, wasn't going to end this in a way that didn't cut him to the quick.

"I'm sorry that you went to all this trouble. Like I said, you seem to be a really nice guy. But I've read the files that Tess gave me and all they proved is that you are both total strangers to me and I don't think that is ever going to change."

She nodded to them all, a brittle, brisk nod that spoke of years of military training and an even longer education at the school of hard knocks and bitter disappointment. And then she was gone, disappearing into the shadows of the interior of his home toward the front door.

Roan stepped into his rapidly narrowing field of vision, his expression concerned and apologetic.

"Adam, I'm going to make sure that she gets to the hotel. I think it's just going to take her a little time." He paused, obviously searching for the right thing to say. Roan hesitated and then reached out, clasping Adam's shoulder and giving it a squeeze. "Thanks for this and thanks for finding us."

He nodded to Tess and sauntered off, following Sarina's path. Adam stood there, rooted in place by disappointment, anger, sadness and a bone-deep helplessness that threatened to bring him to his knees.

He had failed them again.

And then Tess was there, her arms wrapped around his neck and her words of comfort spilling over him in a balm that soothed like a summer rain on thirsty ground.

"Adam, it's okay. You knew this wasn't going to be easy. It will be okay."

He leaned into her, briefly concerned that his weight, his need would be too much for her but this was Tess. His Tess. Strong. Smart. His.

And he needed her.

"Tess, tell me you need me. Even if it's a lie. Tell me," Adam rasped against the soft, sweet skin of her cheek, heading for her mouth and the sweet relief her kisses could bring. It was selfish and it was too much to ask but he asked it anyway.

The last thing he heard before he took her mouth was the four words that kept him from falling apart.

"Adam, I need you."

Thirteen

Adam needed her.

Everything that they were about, every rule they had established between them told her to leave, to tell him that he'd be okay and go home. Because if she stayed, this would all be different between them and they would never be able to go back.

But she could never leave him now. Not after seeing the complete devastation on his face, the loss of hope. Adam might be stoic and strong but his bone-deep need to take care of the people for whom he felt responsible made him vulnerable. He hid it well but if you got close enough to see what mattered to him, it was hard to miss.

Tess opened to his kiss, using her own response to calm him, to let him know that she wasn't going anywhere.

He broke it off, looking down at her, his eyes searching for answers that she didn't have.

"Are you scared?" she asked him before she could stop herself. There was only so much she could do to soothe him with her body. Other things needed to be faced head-on. He seemed to know that she wasn't talking about them.

"All the time," he answered, tucking a curl around his finger. "I can't fail, Tess."

"You're not going to fail, Adam." She shushed him with a finger laid across his lips. "I don't know if everything is going to work out exactly like you want it to but you won't fail. We'll find the mole and Sarina will come around."

He shook his head, his dark eyes miserable. "I think she's right. I was selfish to drag them both into this. They were doing just fine without me."

Tess didn't know much but she knew some things and they were going to get those straight right now.

"Adam, maybe Sarina isn't ready but she was wrong about your being selfish. I was the one you hired, remember? I know what motivated you from the start and that wasn't part of the equation."

Adam paused, closing his eyes and clearly rolling things over in his head. He opened his eyes, dark lashes making the amber stand out.

"Are *you* ever scared?"

Tess didn't hesitate with the truth. "All the damn time."

"I need you, Tess."

"Then take me. I'm yours, Adam. You know this." Tess was startled by the words that tumbled out of her mouth but she wouldn't take them back. They were true. They'd been heading toward this place and she guessed that the time was right for them to arrive and figure it out from here. It would probably require another change in the rules and she'd have to come clean about her father but that didn't need to happen right now.

Right now, they just needed to be here for each other.

She let him lead her over to the outside lounger. Built like a huge sectional, there was more than enough room for both of them to stretch out and enjoy each other's bodies under the stars. Tess loved the idea of having each other in the wide open. They had so many things between them most of the time, it was impossible for them to erect barriers when the sky stretched out above them like a never-ending story.

Before she could lie down he stopped her, his gaze traveling over her body in a slow, deliberate glide that made her squirm with anticipation. Adam, focused entirely on her, was something she would never get enough of. It made her feel cherished and beautiful and special. Heady stuff for anyone but since she'd never felt this way before, it dug under her skin and buried itself somewhere scarily close to her heart.

As if he could read her mind he said, "You're so beautiful, Tess."

"You make me feel beautiful, Adam."

He nodded, his gaze drifting down to where his fingers were undoing the tiny buttons on her sundress, his skin grazing the sides of her breasts. She wasn't wearing a bra and the sensation of his flesh, warm and rough against her, was intoxicating.

"I love the way we look together," he murmured, his fingers slipping under the fabric to stroke her right nipple. Tess arched into his touch, squirming under his attention as her belly grew warm and her sex grew wet with lust. She could barely think about the question with him touching her like that. "Let me see all of you, Tess."

He slid the dress off her shoulders, helping it along as it slid down her body and pooled at her feet.

"Are you cold?" he asked, a wicked smile twisting his lips as he put a finger in her mouth, taking it out when it was good and wet and circling her nipple with it, then leaning over to gently blow on it. She shook her head, biting on her lower lip when he angled his neck to look at her from his position. He was teasing her, eating up every reaction, every moan, every frantic pulse of her heartbeat. "I'll warm you up soon enough."

Adam took two steps back, maintaining eye contact as he toed off his shoes and socks, and quickly removed all of his clothes. Tess took the time to admire his body, strong and lean, his dark skin dusted by silky black hair across his pecs. If she was beautiful, he was…decadent, delicious, the cause of every angel's fall from grace.

"I need you." Adam stepped forward again, kneeling down to remove her sandals, reaching up to lower her panties down her legs, before standing and pressing his body against the length of her own. Tess reached out, a tentative touch to his cheek, needing the physical connection with him right now. "Do you know why?"

She shook her head.

"It's because when I look at you, none of this matters anymore. All the pressures at work, the mole, my family… None of it matters because I see you and I can breathe again."

Adam reached out to her, drawing her down to the lounge cushions, settling over her with his body, his face blocking out the sea of stars shining just over his shoulder.

"I asked you here because I need you to make it disappear. You're the only thing I want to see for a while and then I can do what I have to do." He reached down, his fingers toying with a curl, wrapping it around his finger. "Does that make sense?"

Tess understood all of it. When you were the one

who always needed to be on, to have all of the answers you needed a refuge. They had become that to each other. Somehow in all this insanity and secrets and half-truths, they had become a safe place.

She sat up, pressing her lips to his, filling every soft glide of her tongue with what she was feeling but would not say. Could not say with the secrets she held between them.

"Just look at me. I'll make it all disappear. It will just be the two of us. We'll forget it all together."

Adam's eyes were hot and needy as he stared down at her, his erection lying hot and heavy against her abdomen. She was wide open, as vulnerable as she had ever been and pouring everything into this moment with him.

"Just keep looking at me."

Tess reached down between them, closing her hand around him, squeezing and stroking until he writhed under her touch. His breathing was ragged: rough, needy and raw.

"More. Please. More." He groaned, writhing under each stroke of his erection. His head dipped down, fingers clenching on cushions at the sides of her body, knuckles white and body shaking with his desire. He was gorgeous, skin smooth and damp with sweat, heavy on top of her. "Jesus, Tess. More."

Adam suddenly gathered her close to him, flipping them both over so that she now hovered over him. Tess threw her head back, letting the starshine rain down over her, coating them both with its power. When she looked down at Adam he was smiling, tracing up and down her sides with the back of his hands.

"You're a witch, Tess Lynch. You cast your spell and I've never gotten away from it."

"You're not the only one under a spell, Adam Redhawk. What did you do to me?"

"If you figure it out, let me know. I'll keep doing it."

He leaned up and kissed her, deeply and thoroughly, ramping up the tension between them with the twist and tangle of tongues. Adam released her mouth, lifting slightly to trail his lips down her neck, across her collarbone, and into the valley between her breasts. Tess braced herself over him, hands on each side of his shoulders as he took his time with each breast, suckling and licking at each hard nipple until she squirmed against him.

Tess straddled him wider, her slick center rubbing along the hard, hot length of him. It reminded her of evenings in the back seat of cars with boys, not willing to go all the way but enjoying the buildup and anticipation of how good two bodies could feel together. This was better. She knew how good it was going to be with Adam.

"Adam, I need *you*. Now."

She reached down between them, taking him in hand and dragging the head of his penis against the swollen folds of her sex. It felt so good, the tip sliding inside her, then the rest of him following inch by inch. She slid down his length, gasping with the fullness of him. He was so hard, so thick. Tess stroked her hands over his chest, enjoying his masculinity. The glide was so sweet, so easy as she rode him at a gentle pace, drawing out the pleasure as long as she could.

Adam fell back onto the cushions, his body arching, meeting every one of her downward slides with an answering upward thrust of his own. He pulled her down to him, kissing her deeply as they rode each wave together, their bodies undulating in a syncopation that dragged them higher and higher with each hot, slick, hungry ride.

"Tess, wait." Adam froze, his fingers digging into her hips, holding her in place. His face was strained, teeth grinding against each other. "I have to go get a condom."

"But you feel so good, Adam." She would kill Mia if her sister were to do what she was contemplating but here she was. "I'm on the pill. Nothing on my last blood test a couple of months ago. I've never gone without a condom and I'm not sleeping with anyone else."

He stared at her, the wheels spinning as he weighed the decision between them. When he spoke, it was direct, clear. "I tested negative for anything three months ago. I've not had anyone since then but you, and I'm not sleeping with anyone else."

She nodded, heart pounding with the weight of this decision. But she wouldn't go back. She didn't want to go back.

She was not safe with this man. She wanted to protect him, to comfort him, to be with him. He'd worked his way inside her heart and she'd done nothing to stop him. It was as if she was finally acknowledging why she was here now, why she'd agreed to this fling in the first place. It hadn't been just sex. It hadn't just been an itch to scratch.

Adam is it for me. He could be the one for me.

She traced the contours of his face, his cheekbones, his eyelids, his lips, and then ran her fingers back up to lightly caress the dark shadows underneath his eyes. Adam reached up, grabbed her hand and pressed a kiss onto the palm. The sweetness of the gesture, combined with the fullness of his body deep inside her made her breath catch, her heart actually skip a couple of beats.

"I need you, Tess. I want you so much." His gaze caught her own in a stare of unflinching unapologetic need and desire. "I've wanted you since the beginning."

"Adam."

"I want you, baby. Come on, you know I can make it good for you."

Adam pulled her down again and kissed her, his

tongue thrusting inside with a brutal, possessive hunger that overcame all of her senses. This was possession, ownership, laying claim. The point of no return. But she claimed him back, so glad to know that she wasn't alone in this. They needed to know that they weren't alone in this; they had each other.

Their bodies moved together, beginning a slow rise and fall, an easy rhythm that would get them both there eventually. No rush. Nowhere to be except here with each other.

She sat up, bracing herself on each side of his shoulders, eyes locked on each other as they gave and took from each other. Tess was so wet, her body gripping him on each stroke. The loss was acute every time he pulled out and built the hunger again with every thrust back in.

I want you.

I need you.

I love you.

Their bodies said everything that neither of them was willing to say tonight. It was enough that they were honest with each other about what this was, what it had become. It would be impossible for them to go backward. Adam knew it. She knew it. But they'd jumped off that cliff together and would figure it out later. It might be something. It might be nothing. It might be forever. But none of that would be settled tonight.

Her orgasm was on her before she realized it. Sudden and powerful, it wrenched a long, deep moan from Tess that she shouted into the open air, hearing its faint echo as it bounced along the ravine below. Adam groaned beneath her, his fingers grasping her hips as he thrust upward, once and twice and then three times. He came then, deep inside her as she collapsed against him.

Their bodies were slick against each other, sticky with their efforts, boneless and heavy as they sank deeper into the cushions of the lounger. Tess couldn't move, didn't want to move as she came down from her high, happy to be where she was and with the man who made her feel safe and wanted. Adam clung to her, large arms wrapped around her body, the aftershocks of their pleasure causing him to shiver against her.

Tess shifted a little, moving her head so that she could look at him. He met her eyes, his sleepy but satisfied.

"Are you cold? Do you want to go inside?"

She shook her head. "Let's stay here a while. Under the stars." And then she remembered what he'd said to her that night at the Lick Observatory. He'd been talking about his lost family but for her this sky would hover over only two people: Mia and the man in her arms. "I just want to lie under the same stars that shine down on the people I love."

Fourteen

She found him.

She yelled in triumph, so glad to be in her home office and not the spaces at Redhawk/Ling. Her shout would have had the security guards running to see what the hell was going on.

Tess fumbled with the keyboard, her fingers trembling with excitement as she pressed the keys to print the information displayed on her screen. She didn't need to print it, everything she'd been searching for was right there on the screen but she was so panicked that it would all disappear that she needed to get it in her hands. On paper. Not just pixels on a screen.

She picked up the phone, hitting speed dial for a number she knew by heart anyway. The line rang and rang, the ringtone shrill in her ear, but there was no answer and the system eventually clicked over to Adam's voicemail. She could have pressed the code to skip his message but she loved hearing his voice, a little awkward but very, very sexy in its directness.

This is Adam Redhawk, CEO of Redhawk/Ling. Leave a message. I'm not great at checking my message so if this is urgent, call my office and leave a message with Estelle. She always knows how to reach me.

She'd already called and left a message with Estelle and sent him a text with no reply so she'd have to wait to deliver the news that she'd found the mole and who he was working for. It was information that Adam would need to protect Redhawk/Ling and it would also be something she could use for her own purpose. She would see him tonight—they had a date to attend one of those fancy-schmancy fund-raiser events at the Nestledown Retreat and she could tell him the news then if he didn't call back sooner.

She grabbed the paper from the printer, scanning the words and data, marking the most important parts with a highlighter. The mole had all of the skill sets necessary to hack into any system and undermine the launch of the app so finding him at this critical point was momentous. It had taken her until the eleventh hour, but it was still momentous.

And he was also someone who could help her. Adam and Justin were reluctant to discuss the act of pressing charges against the person who was trying to sabotage their company. Making those kinds of headlines so close to the launch would pull the focus off their business and place it all on the company. And exposing the fact that you had been susceptible to a hack was never a good look for a tech company.

But the guy would absolutely lose his job and an unemployed man would be a desperate man and a desperate man would be vulnerable to job offers that highlighted his particular skill. Tess needed a hacker to get the final information on Franklin Thornton to expose him as the thief and destroyer he really was. And now she had one.

Pushing back her chair, Tess strode across her office and pulled out the box where she kept everything she knew about Franklin Thornton and her father. Folders and files, papers yellowed with age, stained with late-night coffee, and likely some tears. Some shed in grief and many more shed in anger. Tess let out a huff of air as she flipped through the stacks and stacks of papers—some of which she'd memorized—as she searched for that fury, the blinding rage that usually asserted itself when she indulged in these walks down memory lane.

It was all here on the table: years of instances when Franklin had taken advantage of people a lot like her father. Franklin didn't just play games with men and women of his same stature and wealth and power; he played with those who were less than him, taking their dreams from them when he wanted what they had. And he never cared about what happened to them. He never gave them another thought when he'd taken from them everything they had of value.

Franklin hadn't cared when he'd destroyed her dad. And he hadn't even cared enough to see Michael Roberts's daughters when they'd gone to him to beg for help. Both she and Mia had been turned away, hadn't even gotten past the administrative assistant.

So why was she hesitating now when she almost had him in the crosshairs?

Tess knew why. Adam Redhawk.

She pulled out the chair nearest the table and slumped down into it. She was tired, exhausted and queasy and wanting desperately to go back to bed. Tess touched her forehead, wondering if the infection from three weeks ago hadn't fully cleared up but she had felt fine after a few days of rest and all of the antibiotics. In truth this was probably related to the long days and even longer nights she'd been spending with Adam since the night of the dinner with this family.

That night had transformed everything between them, turned the entirety of their arrangement completely upside down, and she'd never been so happy and so scared in her whole life.

That wasn't true. She'd been terrified, bone-deep cold with fear, when she'd suddenly had to face raising Mia all by herself.

But this fear was something different; this was risking it all. To do this with Adam, to give in to what she felt for Adam would mean giving up this vendetta against Franklin. Not because she was worried that Adam would be implicated in any of it but because it would hurt him.

There was no love lost between Adam and his adoptive father but that didn't matter when it came to Adam and his huge heart. He took responsibility for the people in his life, carried so much of their burden as his own and this would be a blow she couldn't bear to see him take.

Adam's strength, his need to take care of everyone, was what made him survive the childhood in Franklin Thornton's house. He had needed to get through it so that he could find his family someday. He had needed to succeed at school and in his company so that he could take care of his employees. He'd paid for her to do anything necessary to find his siblings because he carried the guilt of having let them down.

If she exposed Franklin, she would hurt this man.

A man she wanted to protect because of what he did for everyone else.

A man she was falling for.

In frustration she grabbed the files on the table and shoved them back into the box. She couldn't believe that she was seriously contemplating giving up on her father for the son of the man who destroyed him. But Adam was a decent, good man in spite of what had happened to him. He was sexy and funny and smart and he needed her. He wanted her.

And no one had ever made her feel like she was enough.

That just having her in their life would be enough.

Tess squirmed in her chair, her stomach clenching with nausea that made her gasp with the intensity of the feeling. She checked her watch and realized that it was midafternoon and it had been many hours since she'd eaten a bagel along with her coffee.

Heading to the kitchen, she took a mental inventory of the contents of her fridge: leftover Chinese, cold pizza, yogurt, eggs. The eggs made her smile, thinking of the omelet Adam had made her when she was sick. It had been surprisingly decent; nothing that was going to get him on the Food Network but it was good, filling when she'd needed it.

She opened the fridge and grabbed the carton of eggs, butter and cheese and placed them on the island counter. Tess shifted to the coffee maker, popping in a cup and turning it on to perk while she threw some bread in the toaster. Soon the smells of melting butter and coffee filled the air as she worked at the cooktop and her mouth watered at the thought of breakfast for supper. It was one of her favorite things to cook, remembering many meals with Mia where bacon and eggs filled their bellies.

Her mouth watered again and her stomach rolled

with another wave of nausea. Tess leaned heavily on the counter, breathing in deeply through her nose and pressing a trembling palm against her stomach. A cold sweat broke out between her shoulder blades, streaking down her back and her arms and along her scalp.

Tess turned off the burner and bolted to the bathroom, flinging up the toilet seat as she fell to her knees in front of it and emptied everything out of her stomach. She heaved, every muscle straining as she wretched, her nails digging into the palms of her hands. Finally, minutes that felt like an hour later, she slumped back against the side of the tub, legs extended on the tile floor. The chill of the porcelain seeped through her leggings and made her shiver.

It had to be the sickness back again but even during the worst of it she hadn't felt this bad, hadn't thrown up like she drank too much of the grain alcohol fruit punch at a fraternity party.

Tess stood and moved towards the sink, splashing cold water on her face. She felt better but not completely settled so she dried off and opened up the medicine cabinet, reaching for the Tums when the box of tampons caught her eye. She paused, shaking her head at the random thought that skittered across her brain and reached for her phone. It was crazy. Impossible.

Tess tapped the app that tracked her cycle and the

dates on the display made the ball of anxiety in her gut expand to rivers of ice running under her skin.

She closed the app, slid her finger across the screen and searched for Mia's number. She was visiting for a long weekend, out running errands, and Tess might be able catch her in time.

She pressed the number for her sister and when she answered, asked for what she needed and settled in to wait.

The quickness of Mia's footsteps on the floorboards gave away that she was running at a clip.

Tess couldn't help herself. "Mia, I've told you a million times not to run in the house."

Her sister's face was ruddy with excitement and concern as she skidded to a stop in the doorway of the bathroom. "Tess, if you call me and tell me to pick up a pregnancy test or two on my way home and you expect me not to run? You are out of your mind."

"Fine. Fine." Tess waved off her arguing and held her hand out for the test. "Just give it to me, please."

Mia paused a moment, eyes locked on hers, and Tess had to look away to avoid the pain and confusion swimming in them. She didn't see disappointment there, not yet; she wasn't sure she could handle that right now.

The drug store bag rustled, the box was placed in her hand, and the door shut behind Mia with a gentle click. With shaking hands, Tess opened the package and followed the directions. When she was done, she opened the door and went to find Mia, taking the stick with her.

Her sister was on the couch, huddled with her knees pulled up to her chest. She glanced down at the stick, eyebrows raised in question.

"I have to wait a couple of minutes," Tess replied, slipping down on the sofa and easing down to lean on Mia's shoulder. "I don't want to wait alone."

The moments slid into each other, feeling both forever long and speeding by at the same time. Tess refused to look at the stick, refused to stare it down in a feeble attempt to get it to reveal its secret sooner rather than right on time. Mia fidgeted beside her, her distress advertised with every crossing of her legs and deeply troubled sigh.

"Do you want a baby?" Mia asked, her fingers plowing through Tess's curls.

What a question. What a question she didn't have an answer for.

"I've never thought about a baby." She spoke with conviction but that was a lie. She'd thought about children but only in the context of something she'd never have—along with a marriage. She'd raised Mia and she had an all-consuming purpose to see her father done right, and none of that left room for fantasies about commitments and children she was never going to have. "This wasn't planned. Antibiotics and unprotected sex." She cut a stern glance at her sister. "I knew better. I should have done better."

The next question came in a small voice, a tentative inquiry mumbled into her shoulder. "Would you keep it?"

"Yes." She answered before she thought about it but the answer felt right, was right. It would be a complete rocking of her world and she doubted that she would be very good at it but the answer would be yes. "I didn't screw up too badly with you. I think I could do it."

"What would Adam do? Does he want a family?"

Now *that* was the question. And she had no idea of the answer. He was a natural family man, a loving and caring brother, even though he thought he was a failure.

And he had quickly become the one person she would take a chance with, the person she trusted to take a risk.

She glanced at her watch and it was past the time for the stick to tell her future, like the psychic woman at the carnival. But instead of getting a bunch of cryptic premonitions about meeting a dark-haired man, this wouldn't be hocus-pocus. It would be the definitive end result, the end game, the final score. No wiggle room. No multiple interpretations.

And if the result of the test told her that she was carrying Adam's child could she still use the information sitting in her office to take down his adoptive father?

Adam would be thrilled, vindicated, and relieved to be told about the mole. But she had no idea if he'd be as thrilled to be a father. For a woman who had spent so much of her life avoiding unnecessary complications, she'd created a Rubik's Cube mess of her life. Making up for lost time, she supposed.

Tess reached out, pausing to squeeze the shakes out of her fingers, finally grasping the long white plastic stick and looking at the answer.

"Well," she said, swallowing hard and reaching out to take Mia's hand. "Isn't that something?"

Fifteen

"I was right."

Adam leaned in close to whisper into Tess's ear, brushing a soft kiss against the sweetest spot on the back of her neck as they walked into the gala to benefit the children's hospital. Held at the exquisite Nestledown Retreat, it was one of his favorite venues if he was forced to attend a five-thousand-dollar per plate dinner and endure hours of small talk with people who'd never made him feel like he belonged. Surrounded by magnificent redwoods and twinkle lights, it felt like they were walking across the starlit sky.

But nothing compared to how stunning Tess looked tonight.

"*Of course* you were right. Exactly what were you right about *this* time?" She stopped and turned into his arms, the brush of her fingers against his skin a brand of the sweetest fire. Damn, this woman.

But her touch wasn't just flirtatious. She was nervous about something and looking to bolt. He contemplated trying to cajole it out of her but Tess was the keeper of secrets and she'd let him know what was going on when she was ready and not a minute sooner. He was sure it had something to do with the call he'd missed and the message she'd left with Estelle. When he'd tried to call her back, his calls had gone to voicemail. Getting here tonight had been a whirlwind to the extent that he'd had to send a car for her and meet her at the event. But now she was here and he was looking forward to the time when they could talk about whatever was on her mind. He tightened his grip on her and pulled her closer, dipping his head to make eye contact.

"You *are* the most beautiful one here tonight."

And she was. He'd never be able to adequately describe her dress—computer chips and algorithms were his preferred language—but the deep purple of the fabric dipped low in the front and back and exposed mouth-wateringly tempting expanses of her pale skin. Adam couldn't wait to take it off her later. Slowly, very slowly.

"Adam, you need to stop being so sweet," she

murmured, the shadows of the evening doing nothing to hide her blush. "I'll get spoiled."

"I think you deserve to be spoiled. Don't you?"

That spooked her. Her eyes went wide and the nervous fidgeting was back. Hell, this whole situation had him waiting for the other shoe to drop so he didn't stop her when she moved out of his arms. They'd moved from virtual strangers to lovers in the span of a few weeks and neither of them had been looking for anything close to a relationship. But they sure as hell were in the middle of one now and he suspected the one time he took this chance was going to break him.

He'd never done anything halfway in his life and he wasn't going to start now.

Adam reached out, laced their fingers together and led her down one of the candlelit paths, deeper into the shelter of the redwoods and away from the burbling voices of rich people pretending to like each other. The time had come for honesty, for showing his cards and betting it all on Tess. On them.

They reached an alcove in the trees and he turned, cupping her face in his hands and kissing her. Slow and deep, pleading and demanding, ending on a whimper that erupted from somewhere deep inside of Tess. Adam leaned back, maintaining their physical contact, his heart kicking in his chest when she reached out and pulled him back in for a kiss. It was hotter, wetter, and he wondered if there was a back exit to this place. Forget talking, they communicated better when it was just skin on skin.

"Tess, come on." Adam wasn't clear what he was asking her. To leave this place right now or to finally let him in and share whatever secret she was carrying around and guarding like the *Mona Lisa*. She hesitated, biting her kiss-swollen lips in an effort to keep her own confidence. "Baby, tell me what's going on. You've got me tied in knots. I can't stop thinking about you. I haven't felt this crazy over a woman since I was a kid and I tell you I don't like it one bit. Throw me a bone. At least tell me I'm not the only fool here."

"Adam, I didn't want this." Tess pressed her fingers to her mouth in a gesture meant to erase what she'd just said. He waited, giving her time. "I know you didn't want this."

"I wasn't looking for it."

She nodded. "No. Neither was I."

"But we're in the middle of it now, aren't we?"

"Yes. We are. And I can't stop thinking about you, either."

Yes. Yes. Adam let out a long breath, feeling the relief all the way down to his marrow. He had no idea where this was going, what they were starting, but it felt good. So damn good. He kissed her again, pouring out all of the feelings he had inside of him but couldn't say right now. One step at a time. One step toward something spectacular with Tess.

His Tess. Somewhere along the way she'd become his.

"Adam." Tess broke off the kiss, and there was something else he couldn't decipher in her eyes. Another secret. She took a deep breath, her hand hovering between them with her indecision. And then she reached out and grabbed his hand and tugged it down until it rested against her belly. "Another something neither of us was looking for."

Adam's brain wasn't catching up. Numbers. Equations. Algorithms. That stuff came so easy to him but this was indecipherable. Like an equation where he didn't know if he was solving for X or Y. He struggled, scouring her face for a clue. Any hint at what he was supposed to understand.

And then it clicked into place and one plus one equaled…three.

"A baby?" he whispered, his fingers flexing against the slippery fabric of her dress.

"I know it's not what you wanted," Tess said, her tone apologetic, her expression wary but determined. Her hand splayed across her abdomen in a gesture that could only be read as protective.

No, this wasn't what he wanted. Family was a problem for him. He didn't have any luck with family; he had no idea how to be a father. But it wasn't fear that had settled in his belly. No, he wasn't afraid. He was confused and scared…and happy. And that made no sense at all but it was the truth.

"I didn't know that I wanted it," he answered, realizing that he was speaking in damn riddles when he needed to be clear. "Until now."

"Really? Are you sure?" Tess asked, her green-gold eyes warming with cautious optimism.

Was he? Wasn't the answer in the fact that he'd hired her to find Roan and Sarina in the first place? That he'd finally acted on the undeniable compulsion he'd had to find his brother and sister? That he'd lain awake at nights tossing and turning with frustration and an emptiness that he could not name? It was a family-shaped hole in his soul and he was ready to fill it.

"Yes. I'm sure." Adam linked their fingers together over her belly and kissed her, soft and full of promise. Laughter bubbled up between them and the heat rising from the tangle of lips and tongues transformed into warm, lazy presses of lips to cheeks, eyelids and mouths. "I'm going to be a father." He pulled back, gazing down on her, a million questions swirling in his mind. "How? When? How do you feel? What did the doctor say?"

"I'm guessing that it was the night on your deck. My birth control was no match for the antibiotics I had to take when I was sick," she said, her voice full of her own speculation. "We'll go next week and you can ask all of the questions, I promise." Tess answered, her smile dimming as her hands skimmed up the lapels of his jacket, her fingertips lightly brushing against his cheek, tangling in the hair at the nape of his neck. The wariness was back in her eyes, matching the deeper shadows along the edge of the alcove where they stood. "Right now I need to tell you some things. I need to tell you the truth."

Unease pooled low in his belly, subduing the joy of the moment and he knew that this was going to be a night of secrets revealed. But he was determined that they would survive whatever was coming. He had a future with Tess and a baby to protect, and he would save them and their future—he'd failed with his own brother and sister but he wouldn't let history repeat itself. Not with this new chance at a full life of his own.

"What is it, Tess? I have to know everything if I'm going to protect you. Protect us."

"Adam, you have to understand that I didn't know you before." Tess lightly pressed a finger against his lips when he tried to speak again. "Before I knew what kind of man you are. Before I knew that you're not Franklin Thornton's son in any way."

"He's my son. Don't you forget it." As if Tess had summoned him by just speaking his name, Franklin emerged out of the darker spaces on the path, his grin flashing white and feral in the dim lighting. "And you, Tess Roberts, are your father's daughter."

Sixteen

She flinched at the sound of her own name.

For so many years she'd been careful to only use and respond to the name she'd adopted after her father had died. A name borrowed from her grandmother, so not entirely a lie. Or so Tess had told herself.

But the cloud of confusion and suspicion on Adam's face shook her confidence in the deceit she'd been living for the past few years. But in spite of his doubt, Adam was the man he'd proven himself to be over and over. He faced his father, his body shielding her from the threat that now polluted the air. The gesture turned her veins to ice because when he found out the truth, he'd realize that she was the poison.

"Franklin, what do you want?"

"I don't want anything from you, son. I actually have something for you." Franklin smiled and the slight sundown chill in the air turned icy on Tess's skin. She shivered, and when Adam pulled her closer, her heart cracked a little.

"I really don't give a shit." Adam turned to her, his hand sliding against her own, giving her a squeeze and an encouraging smile. "Come on, baby. Let's go home."

"Adam." Tess tried to pull out some semblance of a smile but she didn't have it in her. The happiness of the last few moments still lingered and she used it to give her the strength to do what she needed to do. "My name *is* Tess Roberts…or it was. I did have it officially changed a few years ago."

"I'm really confused right now." Adam shook his head but he didn't let go of her hand and she took that as a good sign. A hopeful sign.

"After my father died, I changed my name. Our name… Mia did it too. We needed a change from… well, we just needed a change. To start over."

"I get that. You had been through so much," Adam tried to soothe her but it made her feel only worse, like the liar she'd been for the past few months. It was time to be honest with Adam and herself.

"My dad was Michael Roberts and he died of an alcohol-induced broken heart after your father took from him the only thing he ever really loved. I only got through it because I had to raise Mia and I was fueled by hate and revenge and the single-minded goal to destroy the man who'd taken my father from me."

"Franklin Thornton."

"Yes. Franklin. The man who raised you."

"And why didn't you tell me sooner?" Adam asked but she could already see that he knew the answer. He just wanted to hear it from her.

"Because she planned to destroy me through you, son. Don't you get it?" Franklin was enjoying this moment; his arms were crossed over his chest and the closest thing he had to a smile twisted his expression into something ugly. In that moment Tess saw her father's face; he'd often worn the same look of hatred but he'd ultimately aimed more of it at himself than at Franklin Thornton. "It was never about you. She was using you."

She focused her attention back on Adam. He was the only one who mattered right now. She'd already wasted too much time on Franklin and her dad.

"He's right, Adam. I was using you." Adam let go of her and she scrambled not to panic. This couldn't be the end. It couldn't. "I *was* using you. Until I fell in love with you."

"Love? You just told me that you were using me to destroy Franklin and you expect me to believe that any of this was about love?"

Tess jumped, the razor-sharp edge of Adam's voice making the first deep cut. But she kept talking because this was the most important thing she was ever going to say in her life.

"Yeah, it ended up being all about love. I fell in love with you and I'd given up on what had brought me to you. Given up on getting back at anyone. Given up the hate and the revenge and living in the past. I fell in love with you, Adam. You replaced *all of that* for me." Tess wiped her eyes, not even realizing until that moment that she was crying. "And I was going to tell you. I was just starting to tell you when…"

"When Franklin beat you to it." Adam was stoic, hard and chiseled under the twinkle lights. "How many chances did you have to tell me the truth? All the time we worked side by side in my office? Any of the times you had access to every goddam thing about me? The times you slept in my bed? You had a million chances Tess and *you* let me learn this from *him*."

Adam's voice cracked on the last word and his expression crumbled. The cold lump that had settled into her chest shattered into a million pieces, the sharp edges making her bleed on the inside. And just as quickly his face was steeled into his usual mask of control. All of the kindness she'd come to love was gone. And she'd seen this face on Adam before; it was the face of the six-year-old boy in his adoption folder.

She'd never forgive herself for being the reason for that expression on his face. To be one more name on the list of people who had betrayed the trust he guarded so fiercely.

"Adam, *you have* to believe me." She was begging. She'd do anything to make this right.

And she had the information to turn the tables on this entire situation at her disposal. She had the name of the mole and the person who was backing the traitor but she couldn't reveal that in front of Franklin. It might be the only chance Adam had to protect Redhawk/Ling and she couldn't take away his right to determine when and where he was going to use the information. She couldn't reveal that in front of Franklin.

That would be the ultimate betrayal.

So she just stared at him, begging him with her eyes to not turn away from her now.

But all the affection and connection they'd had was gone and all that was left was the cold, dark emptiness of the chasm she had created.

"I don't have to do anything for you right now." Adam stared at her for a few seconds and then he turned to walk away.

And then he was gone, becoming one of the shadows surrounding the redwoods, and she was left alone with Franklin. The last two standing; it made sense that they were here together. They'd been bound by toxic tethers for more than a decade.

Franklin moved into her tear-blurred field of vision, triumph in his eyes.

"The next time you want take somebody down, Ms. Roberts, strike first."

Seventeen

"**Y**ou're pregnant. You need to take better care of yourself," Mia said.

Tess paused in the task of dismantling all of the material she'd been obsessively working on for as long as she could remember. Photographs, notes, printouts—everything was going in the trash.

"I just got up early. I always get up early." It was a lie. After arriving home from the gala, she'd taken off her beautiful dress and slid into the cocoon of her bed. She'd hoped for some comfort in the dark but sleep had been impossible and after hours of tossing and turning she'd given up the pipe dream of sliding into the oblivion of unconsciousness and come downstairs to her office. Tess glanced at Mia and then at the clock. "You're not usually up this early. Why are you here?"

"Oh, I don't know. My big sister is knocked up by the son of the man she's been hell-bent on destroying for the past ten years and she's also fallen in love with the guy but he doesn't love her back and now her heart is broken."

"I never said anything about being in love or broken hearts."

"I'm not an idiot. I know what's been going on here even if you don't want to admit it to yourself." Mia snatched the papers from her hand, read them and tossed them into the shredder. "Are you impersonating Marie Kondo?"

"Mia, you are *not* bringing me joy right now."

"Well, then what will bring you joy? Huh? What are you going to do?"

A night of restless sleep was catching up with Tess and she slid into her chair, tossing the papers in her hand across the desk. Her office was a disaster—it matched the hellmouth her life had become.

"I thought that was obvious. I'm ending this vendetta. Absolutely nothing is going to happen. I'm busted. Franklin and Adam have me on their personal most wanted list."

"But you're pregnant."

Tess placed a hand on her abdomen, still amazed. "I am."

"And you love him."

"I really do." And God help her, she did. "Not that it matters now. I betrayed Adam. I lied to him and as far as he's concerned, I'm in the same exact category as Franklin now. I really fucked it up."

Mia was shaking her head like Tess was the dumbest human on the planet. "Then unfuck it." She leaned forward, chin resting on her hand as she scrutinized her sister and the mess surrounding her. "Do the job he hired you to do. Then work on the rest."

"I'm trying."

"Really? To me it looks like your shredding and wallowing."

"I've tried to call Adam. He sends me straight to voicemail and even Estelle is ignoring me. A couple of guys from Redhawk/Ling delivered the personal items I had in my office here to the house." She was frustrated and her raised voice echoed off the walls of the room. "I'm trying to do my fucking job."

"No. You're trying to get the guy back. That's not the job. And the Tess I know would never let voicemail and a cold shoulder keep her from doing the job."

"Do the job…" Tess considered what Mia was saying. She had all of the information, the stuff Adam had paid her to find out about the person who was threatening Redhawk/Ling. And that person was still out there. She needed to put aside her broken heart and do the work she was hired to do. That meant getting her client the information he needed to save his company. She stood, tucking the relevant file in her bag. "I'm going to do my job."

Mia clapped. "And get the guy back?"

Tess rolled her eyes. "One thing at a time, Mia. One thing at a time."

She wasn't here to get the guy back.

That's what she kept telling herself. It wasn't that she didn't want to get Adam back, to erase all the lies that she'd let keep them apart and get back to the place where he looked at her like she was the beginning and the end of his world. What she wouldn't give to once again hear the awe in his voice and the tenderness in his touch when he realized he was going to be a father. Her favorite pair of heels to whoever got her the chance to taste his kiss, to have his hands on her again.

But one look at his face and she knew that wasn't how it was going to go down today.

She'd taken advantage of the night guards and breezed past them with a wave and a determined stride to the elevators. Once she'd arrived on his floor, Tess marched past his secretary, ignoring the gobsmacked expression on Estelle's face and giving her no chance to call security or warn Adam. The only advantage she had was surprise and she used it to get into his office and shut the door behind her. The stupid glass walls ensured that everyone could see the show but Tess was beyond caring and she knew she was on borrowed time.

"Tess, what are you doing here?" Adam rose from his chair, his posture rigid, hands fisted at his sides. Dark shadows under his eyes testified that he hadn't slept last night and that gave her courage.

"You hired me to do a job and I finish what I start."

He was already shaking his head. "No. I'm pretty sure I fired you last night when I learned that you've been lying to me for months. We have nothing to say to each other."

That pissed her off. "Considering that we're going to have a baby together, I'd say we have a hell of lot to talk about in the future but that isn't what I'm here about." Tess moved toward him, ignoring the couch where not so long ago Adam had made love to her. She'd help save his company and then she'd save their future. "You hired me to find the mole and I did it."

That got his attention. He moved from behind the shield of his desk and met her in the middle. He kept her at more than arm's length but he was listening and that was good. "You did? When?"

"It all came together right before the fundraiser but I didn't want to tell you in front of Franklin," she answered, reaching into her bag to pull out the file with everything she'd found. Tess shifted toward the table, spreading out the papers, notes and screenshots. "The guy who tried to do all of the damage is a software engineer named Mitchell Weiss. He was an easy mark with school debt and a sick mom. Couldn't have been a more textbook case as far as finding your weak link. He needed the money, end of story."

"Well, it's certainly the end of his story here at Redhawk/Ling. He's gone," Adam said, his voice low and tense as he moved closer, taking a good look at her file. She tried not to notice how careful he was not to touch her. Tess wasn't going to debate whether Adam should give this guy another chance with him, that wasn't the most important fact on the table.

"The part you don't know is who was paying him." Tess pulled out a series of unencrypted emails, pointing to the highlighted email address. "I think you'll recognize the name. It's Franklin."

Adam stilled, his focus zeroed in on the paper and Tess waited for the explosion. He had every right to lose his shit and if she knew him at all he'd be pissed at himself for not realizing who it was from the beginning.

But the detonation didn't happen. Adam was silent as he bowed his head, hands braced against the surface of the table, everything about his posture signaling defeat instead of defiance. She dipped her head, trying to catch his eye and get some clue as to what was going on in his head.

"Adam?"

"Am I going to have to fight him for everything

for the rest of my goddam life?" When he lifted his head, his dark eyes were blazing with pain and anger and a million unanswered questions. "I don't understand his determination to destroy everything that is mine. Franklin never wanted me so I don't know why he fights so fucking hard to keep me under his control."

"He wants to keep you under his thumb, there's a difference. A huge difference," she said, reaching out to touch his shoulder before she could stop herself. His body was rigid, hot with his anger, but he leaned into her touch and she let the sensation sink in, saving it for later when he remembered that she'd been his enemy as much as Franklin and never wanted to see her again. "And he only fights so hard because he knows that you don't need him. That you are already more of a success than he can ever be. You're already so much more of a man than he will ever be. A really good man."

Adam's sharp intake of breath racked his frame and Tess moved in closer, their chests brushing, warm breaths mingling, bodies giving in to the pull of gravity and emotions strung tight between them. His dark gaze dropped down to her mouth and she held her breath, praying that he gave in to what was still between them. One kiss and she'd know that she had a chance.

Adam raised his hand, fingertips poised to caress her cheek, to draw her in closer. Tess waited, every part of her screaming for him to shatter this wall between them that she'd built with every lie she'd told to him over the last few months. But he just dropped his hand, eyes losing any tender edge and voice as caustic as acid.

"Being a good man has gotten me nowhere, Tess. What did you call that guy? An easy mark?" He laughed, bitterness stripping it of any joy. "I know what that feels like. It's like I have a target on my back." He motioned toward the door, turning his back on her with a harsh finality. "Thanks for the info. I've got a lot to do to save this launch and my entire company."

"Wait, I've got more," Tess stammered, seeing her window of opportunity closing. "I've got everything you need to end this once and for all. To get the target off your back." Her hand hovered over her bag for the briefest moment but she wasn't sure where the hesitation was coming from. She had what Adam needed to finally break free from his toxic situation with Franklin; what was stopping her? She finally reached in and pulled out the thumb drive and held it out to him. "This is everything I have on Franklin. Every dirty deal, every screw job. There isn't a rule, law or regulation that he didn't feel it was his mission to break. I've got enough to make an investigation by the SEC a foregone conclusion and the downfall of his empire a given."

Adam leveled a look of suspicion at her that would

make a nun confess. "If it's so good why didn't you use it?"

This was the hard question that had plagued her for years and it wasn't until last night that she'd gotten her answer. "Because this vendetta was all I had. My dad died and I was an eighteen-year-old suddenly tasked with raising a younger sister and my hatred and obsession kept the terror away. I think that I thought I had to completely step into my dad's shoes to honor his memory—including his failures and his obsession." Tess scrubbed her fingers through her hair, trying to put into words the early morning epiphany that had almost brought her to her knees. "I grew up with a man who loved his desire for revenge and self-loathing more than he loved me. And it hurt me, so much that I couldn't see any other way to survive except to live his life and hope that it made everything worth it. I got so used to living that way that I was terrified to pull the trigger. If I took down Franklin, I would have had nothing. And I couldn't face it."

"So, if you give this to me—what do you have now?"

Oh, that answer was easy. "I have my business, and Mia and this baby." She laid her hand on her stomach and thought of how his hand had been there only a few hours ago. "And I have a life that I want to build with the man I love. It will be more than enough."

"Tess…"

"Adam, let me say this: I'm so sorry. I got close to you for all the wrong reasons and I didn't care if I was going to hurt you in the process of getting the revenge I thought I needed to be happy. But I got to know you and I started to care about the man who was stuck in the middle of this mess and I fell in love. I fell for the guy who plays drums incognito, and the guy who gives Estelle a gift card to the spa and the afternoon off just because she's had a rough week. I fell for the guy who moved heaven, earth and a crap ton of bureaucrats to find the brother and sister he'd lost. And I fell in love with the man who is trying so hard to make a family with them even though he never got a chance to see what one looks like. I fell in love with you, Adam Redhawk. I love you and I'm happy about the baby and I want a future together but more than anything, I want you to be happy and safe and free from Franklin ever having the power to hurt you again. And I want that for you even if you can never forgive me. That will always be more than enough for me."

"Tess, I don't…" Adam was shaking his head, the resolute sadness on his face worse than the anger she'd witnessed last night.

But she wasn't ready to hear that he didn't want her anymore so she moved quickly, pressing the USB into his hand and a kiss to his mouth. She turned on her heel and left his office before he could end it. The fight for them, for their future, would wait for another day.

Eighteen

"I didn't have enough caffeine for this."

Adam tried to ignore Justin pacing in front of his desk drinking both of their coffees. Answering Estelle's SOS, Justin had arrived just as Tess was leaving. Adam had laid out the truth of his fucked-up life: the baby, Tess's betrayal, the information about the mole, and the key to ending Franklin once and for all.

And she'd been right. It was all here, more than enough to take the man down. Tess had done her job and so much more.

"I was *here* all night. I think I need the caffeine more than you do," Adam murmured, hitting the print command for several selected documents. The machine behind him whirred to life and shot out a treasure trove of career-ending data.

"You act like you're the only one who didn't get any sleep last night." Justin shook his head and took another gulp of coffee.

"Spare me the details of the girl you screwed all night and look at this." Adam grabbed the printouts and thrust them at Justin. "Tess has all the goods on Franklin. It goes back years and years, before I was even adopted."

His partner scanned the sheets, eyes getting wider with each one that he read. He whistled, long and loud. "Daddy Franklin has been very, very busy being a very, very bad boy." Justin looked at Adam. "So, what are you going to do with this? Go to the authorities?"

Adam was already putting on his jacket, gathering documents and shoving them into his briefcase. "No. Some of it is so old they wouldn't touch it and he's got too many people in high places in his pocket to guarantee that it would have the desired result."

"Okay, so what are you going to do with this? The last time I checked, Franklin was still gunning for us and we are two weeks away from release or ruin. We haven't even fired that Mitch asshole!"

"Justin, this is insurance. Leverage." Adam fished his cellphone out of his pocket and swiped the screen. "And we're not going to fire Mitch and tip off Franklin. I'm going to see Franklin now. You get security and IT ready to shut down everything associated with Mitch the minute I send word."

"Wait. Wait." Justin moved with the speed of a man fueled by two large coffees and plucked the phone out of his hand. "Franklin isn't going anywhere. What are you going to do about Tess?"

Adam didn't want to have this conversation. Not right now and preferably not ever. "She lied to me, Justin. Got close to me to get back at Franklin. There is nothing *to do* about Tess. We're done."

"What about the baby?"

"We'll work out arrangements for the baby but the white picket fence and happy family dream you're always talking about isn't going to happen." Adam grabbed his phone back and headed for the door.

"My dream is a week on a yacht with two or three supermodels in my bed and a high-stakes poker game on the offer. I didn't say anything about happy families and fences. *You* were the one dreaming about those things, man." Justin's words hit him in the gut, no they hit higher, right behind his ribcage. "And I heard what she said—"

"You heard? What? How?"

"I picked up Estelle's line and hit the intercom/ listen code." Justin shrugged like it was something he did all the time and Adam made a mental note to have that function disabled on Estelle's phone as soon as possible. "So, I heard everything and all I know is that she's got a lot of guts and she must really love you to give up everything for you."

He scoffed, clearly not having heard the same conversation that Justin did. "She didn't give up anything. Franklin will get what he deserves and she'll get exactly what she wants."

Justin was shaking his head. "You are the dumbest genius I know, so I'm going to say this slow and in as few words as possible." Adam flipped him the bird but he ignored him and kept moving on. "Tess doesn't get *anything* she wants. She doesn't get her father the recognition for his invention. She doesn't get you, the man she loves. She doesn't get to move on and have a little happiness after the crap life she's been dealt." He held up a finger to pause the response hovering on Adam's lips. "Wait, I was wrong, she gets lots of things. She gets *you* being a stubborn asshole and refusing to acknowledge that you love her. She gets *you* making her pay over and over again for trying to survive and make a life of the crap her father put her through. And, this is the best part, she gets to raise *your kid* and hope to God that he or she isn't as stubborn as you are." He made an elaborate play out of counting on his fingers and ended the show with an empty hand, just like a magician. "So, in the end, she really does end up with a whole lot of nothing because she gave you everything—her information, her only chance at vindication and her heart. And I didn't hear her ask you for *anything*."

Justin wasn't wrong. He could be reckless at the poker table, terrible with women and he drove Adam crazy but he was a man who noticed the details. It didn't matter if it was a million numbers on a spreadsheet or a single puzzle piece out of place, nothing got past Justin. And he'd listened to every word that Tess had said, really *heard* her.

"She said she loves me."

"Clearly, she's crazy. I should get her help."

"I'm in love with her," Adam said, knowing that he sounded like an idiot. He didn't care.

"Again, you are the dumbest genius I know," Justin teased, making himself comfortable on the couch. "But you get there eventually."

"She's going to have my baby." Adam couldn't stop the grin from tugging at the corner of his mouth. "I'm going to be a father."

"Yeah, you are." Justin's wide grin was contagious. "And I'm going to be an uncle."

Adam slipped off his jacket and headed back to his desk. "Well, Uncle Justin, I have a plan to save Redhawk/Ling, get Franklin out of our lives forever and to get Tess what she never asked for. You in?"

Nineteen

"Mia, why are we here?"

Tess paused at the double doors leading to the largest conference room at Redhawk/Ling and squinted at the couple dozen people milling about the room. She recognized a number of them, all reporters from local and national news outlets. A small stage and podium were set up on one end of the room, framed by the view of the gorgeous campus through the floor-to-ceiling windows. Adam had the same view in his office and she'd often caught him staring out the window, his mind a million miles away.

She'd heard nothing from Adam since last week when he'd let her walk out of his office. Tess had scoured the news for any word on the mole but all the news that was fit to print was about the launch of the app. Full steam ahead. No complications. No espionage.

And no invitations to meet up and talk about the baby. About them.

She snagged the back of her sister's jeans and hissed into her ear, "I don't think we're in the right place."

Mia pulled out the printed email invite and took another look. "Nope. This is the place."

"This can't be right." Tess couldn't imagine why Justin would have asked them to come to the office and have all these people here at the same time.

When they'd received the email, Tess had presumed that Adam was using Justin as a go-between to discuss the baby, and while that was never going to fly in the long-term, she was willing to take the meeting to get the conversation started. Adam had been radio silent for almost a week and Tess had resolved to give him some space. While the clock was obviously ticking where the baby was concerned, they had time and she didn't want to push. She hoped that Adam would come around and they could have a life together but with each day that passed, it was harder and harder to believe that she would get what she dreamed about. And now, seeing this large gathering made her doubt if Adam even knew she'd been invited today.

"Tess, Justin said that we both needed to be here. He said it was important." Mia wriggled free from her grasp and sauntered into the room with the carefree nonchalance that Tess had possessed just a few short weeks ago. "And it's not like we have somewhere else to be."

That was the truth. Tess had wrapped up a couple of small cases and she'd referred another one to a colleague. Because of the payment for services rendered to Redhawk/Ling, she could afford to turn down a couple of jobs and nurse her broken heart. It was crazy how much she could miss a man who'd been a stranger a couple of months ago.

Tess moved to slide into a seat toward the back, nodding at several reporters she knew from prior jobs just as Estelle approached the small podium and asked everyone to take their seats. The room was at that point where the A/C wasn't keeping up with the mass of body heat and the flush across her skin added to the anxious itch that kept her on the edge of her seat. The rustle and noise of everyone settling into position masked the sound of Adam's entrance but her body went on high alert the second he crossed the threshold.

He was wearing her favorite suit, as midnight black as his hair and slim cut on his athletic build, with a crisp white shirt underneath. He moved like a large cat, smooth and graceful in his individuality, and the beautifully cut suit emphasized every muscle of his body. Adam was a beautiful man, sexy as hell, and several of the reporters murmured their admiration while she bit back the urge to tell them to back away from her man.

Because he wasn't her man. Not anymore.

The sight of Justin and then Franklin Thornton following Adam onto the stage ripped her out of her thoughts. It roused the crowd into a groundswell of murmurs and the flash of cameras highlighted the screen that descended from the ceiling to span the width of the area. Tess tried to get a read off their expressions and while Justin was sedately smug and Franklin was furious, Adam was a cool customer. He was poised and calm as he approached the microphone, his charismatic smile capturing everyone's full attention. She wished that he would notice her but he didn't even look in her direction and she wondered if he even knew she was there.

"Good afternoon, my name is Adam Redhawk and I am the co-owner and CEO of Redhawk/Ling. On behalf of my partner and CFO, Justin Ling, and the President of Trident Investments, Mr. Franklin Thornton, I want to welcome you all to the announcement of an exciting collaboration between our two companies. Since Justin and I started Redhawk/Ling ten years ago, we have been committed to developing and creating innovative products that change the way we live for the better. Trident has been a leader in recognizing and financing projects that started in somebody's garage and those created in a state-of-the-art facility. Together we want to be part of a future that encourages and supports new, fresh and talented inventors to take the risks that create positive change that will impact generations to come. To that end, we are announcing the creation of a program that will recognize the best of the best in new ideas and give them the space, opportunity and the funding to make their dreams a reality. Ladies and gentlemen, I am proud to present to you the Michael Roberts Research Foundation."

Tess gaped in shock as Adam pressed a button on a remote control and a photograph of her father appeared on the large screen behind him. As his words penetrated the confusion and connected with her brain, a slideshow began that featured her father throughout his career, his inventions and finally a photo of their little family, smiling and leaning on each other. Tess didn't bother to wipe at the tears streaking her cheeks, not wanting to miss one of the images on the screen. Mia made a choking sound beside her and reached out to grab her hand, her sister's fingers cold against the suddenly overheated temperature of her own skin. And while Mia's grasp kept her grounded the expression in Adam's eyes as he met her gaze made her heart fly.

Adam paused a beat and then continued, never breaking eye contact with her. "Mr. Roberts was a tireless and brilliant scientist and engineer who was integral to the development of what is now Silicon Valley. Unfortunately, his life was cut short but this foundation will ensure that his enthusiasm, dedication, brilliance and innovative spirit will live on. To that end, Redhawk/Ling and Trident have endowed the foundation with matching grants of ten million dollars each with future opportunities for other companies to join us." Adam gestured toward Justin. "I'm going to hand the Q&A over to Justin Ling."

Tess watched Adam step down from the stage and stride across the room directly to where she sat. His expression was intense, his stride powerful; everything about him telegraphed that he was coming for her. She rose from her seat, poised to meet him eye to eye. If they had any chance to work, it was how it had to be.

He stopped in front of her and held out his hand. "Walk with me, please."

It wasn't a question she had to consider. She would go anywhere with Adam Redhawk.

Tess ignored the murmurs and quizzical looks thrown in their direction but threw a quick look toward Mia. Her sister's thumbs-up and big smile contrasted with her tear-stained cheeks. Mia nodded, giving her blessing as Tess headed out of the room.

They said nothing as they progressed down the hallway from the conference room, up the large, center staircase and past Estelle's desk. Adam opened the door to his office and tugged her inside, shutting it firmly behind them. He turned, his eyes dark as night and filled with enough heat to make her shiver.

"Adam." She gestured toward the conference room full of people. "I don't know what to say. What you did out there—"

"What I did was make things right," Adam said, advancing forward one measured step at a time. Tess wasn't one to run and she stood her ground, her breath quickening when they stood close enough to exchange body heat. His warm, sharp scent surrounded her and she inhaled deeply, drinking him in like a woman dying of thirst after days spent in the desert. "What I did was try to make up for the wrongs committed by Franklin against your father."

"Those are things Franklin did. They are on him and only him. They were not your mistakes to fix."

"Yes, they were." The timbre of his voice, the earnest expression in his eyes told her that he believed it, that he thought what happened was his responsibility. She'd believed the same thing for so many years, convinced that the sins of the father could be levied against the son but she'd been so wrong.

"No. No." She shook her head. "Why would you think that?"

"Because I love you." Adam lifted his hand and cupped her cheek, holding her still so that their eyes remained locked together. It was unnecessary; she would never look away from him as long as he looked at her the way he was looking at her now. "It didn't matter who was at fault. You were hurting and I could make it right. I did it because I love you."

Damn. She'd thought about him saying the words to her more times than she could count and the reality was better than anything she could have imagined.

"And what exactly did you do, Adam?" she asked, reaching out to grasp his lapel and draw him down even closer. His gaze dropped to her mouth and back up to meet her eyes, his lips twisting into a sexy slip of a smile that made her shiver in anticipation. "The foundation. My father… Franklin. What did you do to make that happen?"

"It was very simple in the end. I took copies of the information to Franklin—the file you had on his years of illegal and unethical conduct, the evidence of the mole and his payment for industrial espionage—and told him that I would give it all to the authorities, the SEC, the press, if he didn't help make it right. I made him agree to give the money for the foundation in your father's name. I'm not naive. He doesn't give a shit about the pain he caused or what I think of him, but he lives in mortal fear of losing his power, his company, his reputation. He cares about that more than he's ever cared about anyone, including me." Adam shook his head, his left hand slipping around her hip, settling in the small of her back to drag her body against his. "And I don't care about why he did it. I only cared that this would make everything you've done worthwhile. I wanted to give you and Mia peace." He leaned in, his lips brushing over her eyelids, his large hand lowering to cover her stomach. "I wanted to give us a chance to be a family. A real family."

Tess reached up, grasping his face in her hands and pulling him down to her in a kiss. It was hot and wet and deep and left them both panting and clinging to each other. Adam had given her so much. Now it was up to her to find the words to ensure that he knew how she felt, what she really wanted.

"I love you. And from now on, I will be your family."

Adam's grin was sexy and predatory and the last thing she saw before he took her mouth again in a kiss that started a little sweet but quickly morphed into a deep, dark press of lips and tongues. He groaned, his hands roaming all over her back, her face, her arms, her ass. He lifted her up, walking them both backward until he placed her on the desk. Adam settled between her legs and she moaned when his erection pressed against her core.

Suddenly, there were too many clothes between them; too much space and air and distance. Tess wanted him inside her, needing them to be one in every way that counted. She had his heart, she needed his body, his strength.

She reached for his belt, remembering at the last moment that they were exposed in his office. Anybody who walked by would see them and there were several dozen reporters in the building at this very moment. This might be the time but it wasn't the place.

Tess reluctantly broke off the kiss. "Adam, we can't." He looked confused, lust drunk, and she nodded toward the floor-to-ceiling glass walls of his office. "I don't really want to give any of the press *this* kind of story."

"Oh. Let me show you some of the upgrades I had installed in the office."

She watched as his confusion morphed into the expression of someone who ate not one, but every single canary. He lifted his left arm, tapped on his smartwatch a few times and then blinds began to descend from a hidden place in the ceiling. In less than a minute, the office was enclosed, intimately private.

Tess laughed. "I love this kind of upgrade."

Adam leaned over her, his finger tracing down from her collarbone to the cleft between her breasts. His touch was electric on her skin and she shuddered when he deftly undid the first button on her blouse and grinned his wicked grin.

"So, where were we…?"

Epilogue

Five months later.

"Justin is acting really weird."

Adam wrapped his arms around Tess and pressed a kiss against the bare skin of her shoulder. Tess smiled and leaned back into him, humming contentedly when he covered the baby bump with his hand. At five months pregnant, the morning sickness was gone, her energy was back, and none of her old clothes fit anymore. She really was glowing and her voluptuous body was even more lush and beautiful. She was the sexiest woman he'd ever seen.

Normally she was a complete and total distraction for him, but not right now. His best friend and business partner was *really* acting weird.

"Well, Justin *is* weird," Tess commented, reaching out to snag a carrot stick from the buffet table. "So, isn't that normal for him?"

"I guess so," Adam agreed but he wasn't convinced. "Sarina is acting weird too."

From their position they could view the entire party. It was a family and close friend affair for the gender reveal; an odd mix of all of the people in their lives. Among a couple of dozen other people, Mia and Estelle were there, along with Roan, Sarina and Justin.

And Justin was definitely avoiding Sarina.

And Sarina was avoiding Justin.

"What the hell is *that* all about?" Tess asked, twisting to look at him. "You don't think Justin said something to her?"

"I don't think so. They just met and even Justin can't piss somebody off that fast. It could just as easily be Sarina being her usual grumpy self." Adam watched his sister closely, and while he didn't know her well yet, he knew the difference between her usual I'm-pissed-off-at-the-world-in-general personality and when her dislike was aimed at one particular person.

And Sarina looked like she wanted to murder Justin. Slowly. Painfully.

If Justin had pissed her off, Adam would kick his ass. Sarina had initially declined to attend today but ultimately the universe had intervened and busted the motor on Sarina's Harley. Unsurprisingly, Sarina had refused his offer to pay to have the bike fixed or to buy her a new one and so she was hanging around for a few weeks and working at Redhawk/Ling to get the funds.

He shook it off, turning Tess in his arms and kissing her softly, with a hint of heat and a whole lot of promise for a private celebration later. "But I don't want to talk about them. I want to talk about whether you want a boy or a girl."

"Yes." Tess grinned, refusing to tell him her preference. It was their private joke and now he wasn't sure if he wanted to know. He knew everything he needed to know. He knew that she loved him and that she wanted to create a family together.

It was more than enough. It was more than he'd ever thought he'd have. Adam was slowly making progress with his brother and sister. The years had made them into such different people but they were all in this together, tentatively making memories and reforging bonds. Becoming a family. And now he was going to have a family of his own.

Redhawk/Ling was still riding high after the success of the app launch. The investors and employees were still celebrating the success and the money in their pockets. The Michael Roberts Research Foundation had awarded the first round of grants to promising inventors, with Tess and Mia delivering the first checks in person. They were making a difference in the world.

He had a very, very good life.

"I love you, Tess," he said, nuzzling against her throat before whispering into her ear. "And I want to spend the rest of my life with you. You and me and our baby, forever."

When he pulled back to look down at her, Tess was smiling at him, her cheeks flushed with her happiness. "I love you too. Always."

"Break it up, you two!"

They were interrupted by Mia, bringing over to them the box rigged to reveal the gender of the baby. Adam had been told that they would both tug on the ribbons sprouting from the top of the box and confetti and balloons in either pink or blue would spring into the air. Both of them had thought that the idea was silly but now that the moment was here, Adam was surprised at the rush of excitement bubbling in his belly.

He was going to be a father.

They both reached for a ribbon and Adam leaned over and took Tess's mouth in a quick, hot kiss. He winked at her and gestured toward the ribbons. "On the count of three?"

She nodded.

"One."
"Two."
"Three."

* * * * *

*What's going on
between Justin and Sarina?
Don't miss*
Seducing His Secret Wife
by USA TODAY *bestselling author
Robin Covington
to find out!*

*Available February 2021
from Harlequin Desire.*

WE HOPE YOU ENJOYED
THIS BOOK FROM

⟨H⟩ HARLEQUIN
DESIRE

*Luxury, scandal, desire—welcome to
the lives of the American elite.*

Be transported to the worlds of oil barons, family dynasties,
moguls and celebrities. Get ready for juicy plot twists,
delicious sensuality and intriguing scandal.

6 NEW BOOKS AVAILABLE EVERY MONTH!

#2779 THE RANCHER'S WAGER
Gold Valley Vineyards • by Maisey Yates
No one gets under Jackson Cooper's skin like Cricket Maxfield. When he goes all in at a charity poker match, Jackson loses their bet and becomes her reluctant ranch hand. In close quarters, tempers flare—and the fire between them ignites into a passion that won't be ignored...

#2780 ONE NIGHT IN TEXAS
Texas Cattleman's Club: Rags to Riches • by Charlene Sands
Gracie Diaz once envied the Wingate family—and wanted Sebastian Wingate. Now she's wealthy in her own right—and pregnant with his baby! Was their one night all they'll ever have? Or is there more to Sebastian than she's ever known?

#2781 THE RANCHER
Dynasties: Mesa Falls • by Joanne Rock
Ranch owner Miles Rivera is surprised to see a glamourous woman like Chiara Campagna in Mesa Falls. When he catches the influencer snooping, he's determined to learn what she's hiding. But when suspicion turns to seduction, can they learn to trust one another?

#2782 RUNNING AWAY WITH THE BRIDE
Nights at the Mahal • by Sophia Singh Sasson
Billionaire Ethan Connors crashes his ex's wedding, only to find he's run off with the wrong bride! Divya Singh didn't want to marry and happily leaves with the sexy stranger. But when their fun fling turns serious, can he win over this runaway bride?

#2783 SCANDAL IN THE VIP SUITE
Miami Famous • by Nadine Gonzalez
Looking for the ultimate getaway, writer Nina Taylor is shocked when *her* VIP suite is given to Hollywood bad boy Julian Knight. Their attraction is undeniable, and soon they've agreed to share the room... and the only bed. But will the meddling press ruin everything?

#2784 INTIMATE NEGOTIATIONS
Blackwells of New York • by Nicki Night
Investment banker Zoe Baldwin is determined to make it in the city's thriving financial industry, but when she meets her handsome new boss, Ethan Blackwell, it's hard to keep things professional. As long days turn into hot nights, can their relationship withstand the secrets between them?

SPECIAL EXCERPT FROM

⬡HARLEQUIN

DESIRE

*No one gets under Jackson Cooper's skin like
Cricket Maxfield. When he goes all in at a charity
poker match, Jackson loses their bet and becomes her
reluctant ranch hand. In close quarters, tempers
flare—and the fire between them ignites into a
passion that won't be ignored...*

Read on for a sneak peek at
The Rancher's Wager
by New York Times *bestselling author Maisey Yates!*

Cricket Maxfield had a hell of a hand. And her confidence made
that clear. Poor little thing didn't think she needed a poker face if
she had a hand that could win.

But he knew better.

She was sitting there with his hat, oversize and over her eyes, on
her head and an unlit cigar in her mouth.

A mouth that was disconcertingly red tonight, as she had clearly
conceded to allowing her sister Emerson to make her up for the
occasion. That bulky, fringed leather jacket should have looked
ridiculous, but over that red dress, cut scandalously low, giving a
tantalizing wedge of scarlet along with pale, creamy cleavage, she
was looking not ridiculous at all.

And right now, she was looking like far too much of a winner.

Lucky for him, around the time he'd escalated the betting, he'd
been sure she would win.

He'd wanted her to win.

"I guess that makes you my ranch hand," she said. "Don't worry.
I'm a very good boss."

Now, Jackson did not want a boss. Not at his job, and not in his
bedroom. But her words sent a streak of fire through his blood. Not
because he wanted her in charge. But because he wanted to show
her what a boss looked like.

Cricket was…

A nuisance. If anything.

That he had any awareness of her at all was problematic enough. Much less that he had any awareness of her as a woman. But that was just because of what she was wearing. The truth of the matter was, Cricket would turn back into the little pumpkin she usually was once this evening was over and he could forget all about the fact that he had ever been tempted to look down her dress during a game of cards.

"Oh, I'm sure you are, sugar."

"I'm your boss. Not your sugar."

"I wasn't aware that you winning me in a game of cards gave you the right to tell me how to talk."

"If I'm your boss, then I definitely have the right to tell you how to talk."

"Seems like a gray area to me." He waited for a moment, let the word roll around on his tongue, savoring it so he could really, really give himself all the anticipation he was due. "Sugar."

"We're going to have to work on your attitude. You're insubordinate."

"Again," he said, offering her a smile, "I don't recall promising a specific attitude."

There was activity going on around him. The small crowd watching the game was cheering, enjoying the way this rivalry was playing out in front of them. He couldn't blame them. If the situation wasn't at his expense, then he would have probably been smirking and enjoying himself along with the rest of the audience, watching the idiot who had lost to the little girl with the cigar.

He might have lost the hand, but he had a feeling he'd win the game.

Don't miss what happens next in…
The Rancher's Wager
by New York Times *bestselling author Maisey Yates!*

Available January 2021 wherever
Harlequin Desire books and ebooks are sold.

Harlequin.com

HDEXP1220

Get 4 FREE REWARDS!

We'll send you 2 FREE Books plus 2 FREE Mystery Gifts.

Harlequin Desire® books transport you to the world of the American elite with juicy plot twists, delicious sensuality and intriguing scandal.

FREE Value Over $20
